More Tales
of the
South Carolina
Low Country

More Tales of the South Carolina Low Country

by NANCY RHYNE

JOHN F. BLAIR, *Publisher*
Winston-Salem, North Carolina

Library of Congress Cataloging in Publication Data

Rhyne, Nancy, 1926 —
  More tales of the South Carolina Low Country.

  1. Tales — South Carolina. 2. Legends — South
Carolina. II. Title.
GR110.S6R44 1984 398.2′09757   84-21710
ISBN 0-89587-042-8 (pbk.)

For Garry and Lisa

Contents

Content

More Tales
of the
South Carolina
Low Country

The Ghost of
Edingsville Beach

I N T H E D A Y S prior to the Civil War, when Edisto
Island planters became millionaires from the pro-
duction of sea island cotton, they built and maintained
beach houses on Edingsville Beach, across a tidal creek
from Edisto Island. Edingsville Beach had a wide,
hard-packed sand beach, where whelks, conchs, cock-
les, and other fabulous seashells washed up with each
tide. The houses of the planters faced the sea, and they
all had the same architecture. They were two stories in
height, had a brick chimney on each end, many
windows, and a porch on the beach side.

During the years when the Edisto planters were
accumulating great fortunes, Mary Clark, a daughter
of one of the planters, became engaged to a Captain
Fickling. The engagement was no surprise to Edisto
Islanders, for both Mary and her fiancé were descendants of old island families, and they had been child-
hood sweethearts. So no expense was spared as plans
for the wedding were made, even to the wedding
dress itself, which was handmade with the utmost
attention given to every small detail.

Finally the wedding day was at hand, and the bride,
on the arm of her father, walked under a canopy of
native vegetation, including white yucca blooms,

1

green myrtle branches, and water spider orchids, as she made her way down the aisle of St. Stephen's Church. When the bride and groom were pronounced man and wife, they left the church and stood in the churchyard to receive the guests as they came from the sanctuary of St. Stephen's. The bride and groom spoke to the guests and invited them to a feast that was then being spread on long tables set up on the beach.

Plantation cooks had been working all night and all that day on the platters of food that were placed on the tables. The cooks were good at preparing the food, using prized family recipes that had been handed down generation after generation. Bleak Hall Salad was made of the white meat of a turkey mixed with thinly sliced palmetto hearts and hard-boiled eggs. This salad was served with a vinegar dressing. Other Edisto delights served at the feast included boeuf de chasse, oyster pie, mincemeat, rice cake, ginger pound cake, and syllabub. There were also hog's head cheese and groundnut candy.

Four weeks after the wedding, the groom set sail for the West Indies, and the bride began to look forward to his return almost before the ship was out of sight. It was October, and most of the planter families were still in residence in their beach houses. Usually, they didn't leave the beach houses for their plantations until after the first frost of the fall season.

Each evening, just before sunset, Mary Fickling walked down to the water's edge. She looked out over the cold water and thought of her husband, far from home. Sometimes fog rolled in from the sea, and she pictured his lonely ship in the mist as she thought of all the mysteries of the sea.

On the evening of October 12, the rolls and swells of

2

the sea began to build, and Mary worried about her husband. She knew that his return was overdue, and if an October hurricane was churning the sea, his ship could be involved. There was no warning system for hurricanes then, but somewhere deep inside her she felt that a dreadful hurricane was coming. When she returned to the house, she found that others were also obviously worried about a hurricane. Then someone said that the causeway to the mainland was flooded and a crossing was out of the question.

Within minutes, the hurricane hit Edingsville. The house in which Mary was staying trembled and swayed, and the structure started to give way. Someone yelled "Quick!" but didn't say anything else. And then the members of Mary's family became very quiet and listened. At first there was a great sucking of air, and then there was total darkness as sea water washed into the house. For Mary it was a long night of terror as she struggled to stay alive.

The next morning an eerie calm and bright sun brought a scene that would never be forgotten. Trees were down. Some beach houses sat askew with porches, chimneys, or windows washed away. Heavy pieces of furniture, chairs, and sofas were here and there on the beach, nearly covered in sand. The very land had changed, and the causeway that had been used for many years by Edisto Island planter families was gone.

Mary ran down to the tideline, and beyond the breakers she saw a dark, lumpy form floating in the sea. As it washed toward shore, she saw that it was the form of a man. She ran into the water, and as the form got closer to her, she recognized the body of her husband. With a shuddering cry, she got down into

3

the water and, tears streaming from her eyes, embraced his body in her arms. Mary was to learn later that his ship and all hands were lost at sea.

There are no beach houses now where Edingsville is located, and no reminders of the days when this place was a fabulous resort. Over the decades this beach has been tormented by devilish hurricanes and unusually high tides, and today it is no more than a sliver of sandy beach adjacent to a marsh. But if you travel by boat, you can go from Edisto Island to the place where this beach once reigned as a summer resort for the rich planters of Edisto Island. And it is said that on moonlit nights a young girl can be seen running into the waves and pulling the form of a man up on the shore. This is the Ghost of Edingsville Beach.

Note: Marion Whaley of Edisto Island has taken many boatloads of people to the shore that was once Edingsville Beach. He has seen the ghost of Mary Fickling pull her husband from the breakers.

The Browned-down Hen

SOME PEOPLE would steal the soda right out of a biscuit. Janie was not like that. She wouldn't steal just anything, but she said her hands naturally stuck to one thing in particular, and she couldn't help it. And that thing in particular was Miss Shecklefoot's hens.

Janie was a housemaid for Miss Shecklefoot, who kept some fat hens in her yard. Janie had to walk past the fowl coop on the way to her cabin, and some hens were usually roosting there. Now and then Janie's hand stuck to a hen. And she knew how to grab a hen by the neck so the chicken couldn't make a sound.

When the youth group at Sweet Water Baptist Church announced a picnic social to be held the next Sunday, Janie thought about the basket of food she would take. She could almost taste a hen, "browned down." Janie knew how to brown down a fat hen just right. After the hen had been browned down, there were about two cups of fat left in the pan. Two cups of pure grease. Janie always made corn bread dressing from the fat. Yes, ma'am, Janie thought, when I walk down that trail headed for the church, I'll have a browned-down hen and corn bread dressing in my basket.

When Janie went to work the next day, Miss Shecklefoot told her that one of her favorite hens had been stolen. The hen's name was Miss Smiff. Miss Shecklefoot had given each of her hens a name.

Janie didn't know who had taken the hen. She had never taken one of Miss Shecklefoot's favorite hens, and she knew Miss Smiff well. She was perturbed that someone else had taken a favorite hen. Now Miss Shecklefoot would be watching the fowl coop much more closely, and it would not be so easy for her to lift a hen for the church picnic.

"I'd like to get my hands on the person who took Miss Smiff," Miss Shecklefoot snorted.

That afternoon Dr. Sam, carrying his black bag, stopped by to check on Miss Shecklefoot. He checked her blood pressure every time he was in the vicinity of the plantation.

"Dr. Sam," the heavyset Miss Shecklefoot murmured, "do you have any strychnine?"

"What on earth for?" the physician asked as he sat down on a lovely Chippendale chair.

"I want to poison some of my chickens. That is the only way I know to stop the thieves who are raiding my fowl coop."

"You want to stop them with strychnine?" Dr. Sam was a bit skeptical.

"Yes. That is to say I want to give my hens some poison that wouldn't *kill* them but would sicken someone who ate one of them. Something that would make the thief wish he could die after eating one of my hens."

Dr. Sam rubbed his forehead. Then he tugged at his beard. He pulled a suspender and let it pop on his chest. He got up, opened his medicine bag, and poured a little liquid into a bottle from another bottle.

"Take this," he said, "and put it in the water you give your hens."

Miss Shecklefoot's eyes shone as she took the bottle. "Oh, thank you, Dr. Sam. Now the thieves stealing my hens will get their just reward."

One afternoon toward the end of the week, Janie walked by the fowl coop, where the hens were quietly roosting. She looked back toward the big house, and she couldn't see Miss Shecklefoot anywhere. She opened the gate slowly, went in, and grabbed a hen by the neck, holding it so tightly the hen couldn't make a sound. Then she left the coop and headed for home, running as fast as her legs would carry her.

On Sunday morning, Janie browned down the hen and made corn bread dressing out of the grease left in the pan.

Later, in church, she thought the reverend would never quit preaching. She longed to sample the hen and dressing in her basket under the oak tree. Finally, the reverend ended his sermon by saying, ". . . and the fire in hell is ten times hotter than any fire you know, and it's still a-heatin'."

After the sermon, tables were set up under the cool of the oak trees shading the church. Janie put her browned-down hen and corn bread dressing on a table and her empty basket underneath. The smell of the food is almost as good as the taste is going to be, she thought.

When the meal was finally over, Janie didn't have enough left over for a sniff. Everybody had sampled generously her hen and dressing.

The next morning Miss Shecklefoot asked Janie what she ate at the church picnic. Before she consid-

7

ered what she was saying, she answered, "Browned-down hen."

"Well, I hope it wasn't one of *my* hens," Miss Shecklefoot scoffed.

"Why?"

"Because I poisoned my hens. If anybody ate one of my hens, they would want to die before long."

"What did you poison the hens with?" Janie reached for a chair and eased herself into it.

"Strychnine," Miss Shecklefoot said, smiling.

Suddenly, Janie didn't feel well. Her tongue was thick and her saliva bubbly, and her tummy was rolling around.

"And I poisoned my hogs, too," Miss Shecklefoot added, watching Janie's reaction. "If anyone is tempted to take one of my shoats and eat him, they're welcome."

Janie left the room, staggered through the hall and out of the house. She kept going until she reached her cabin.

Janie's sister, Lillie, met her on the porch of the small house. Lillie told Janie that Elijah, a ten-year-old boy who lived in a nearby cabin, was dead.

"Elijah's dead?" Janie held onto a post that supported the roof of the porch. She thought about Elijah eating the hen and dressing she took to the church feast. And she thought about the poison Miss Shecklefoot had fed her hens. She felt even more ill than before. God was punishing her for stealing the hen.

"And Elijah's sister is sick, too," Lillie said. "It must be the pneumonia."

"No, it isn't the pneumonia," Janie said sadly.

8

"How do *you* know?" Lillie asked.

Janie didn't answer. She was thinking about what she had to do. First, she was going to Elijah's house to see if she could help the family in any way. Then, she was going to confess to the reverend.

Janie arrived at the cabin of Elijah at about the same time as the reverend. The body was on a cooling board inside, and the family was on the porch. Elijah's mother was so glad to see the reverend that she threw her arms around him and asked him to step inside the cabin and comfort her daughter, who was barely alive.

Janie spoke to everyone and then followed the reverend into the sick room. Dr. Sam was there, leaning over the girl, examining her with a stethoscope.

"How is she?" the reverend asked.

"She'll be all right," Dr. Sam said. "She didn't get as many stings as her brother."

"What do you mean, stings?" Janie asked.

"Elijah and his sister got tangled up in a bee gum and got stung by a great number of bees. The bees took their toll with Elijah, but the girl's going to make it," Dr. Sam said.

"But I thought . . ."

Dr. Sam continued to lean over the bed of the sick girl. "What did you think, Janie?"

"I thought Miss Shecklefoot poisoned her hens, and Elijah and his sister ate some of the hen I took to the church."

Dr. Sam turned around. He frowned briefly. "Miss Shecklefoot did ask me for some poison to make the thief of her hens sick. Strychnine, I believe." He sounded vaguely accusing. "But to tell you the truth," he said, winking at Janie, "I just gave her a little sweet water. You know, I had a premonition some of her hens would end up on a table at Sweet Water Baptist Church."

Alice, the Ghost of
The Hermitage

D R . A L L A R D F L A G G moved into his new home,
The Hermitage, on Murrells Inlet, in 1849 and
invited his widowed mother and his sister Alice to live
with him. With delicate features, luminous brown
eyes, and thick auburn hair that hung to her waist,
Alice was a girl of unusual beauty.

Alice had not shown any interest in a beau, but her
older brother Allard was beginning to cast interested
glances toward Penelope Bentley Ward, and her other
brother, Dr. Arthur Flagg, was openly courting Penelope's sister, Georgianna Ward.

The Wards of Brookgreen Plantation were the most
noted of the planter families in the Low Country
during the late 1840s. The amount of rice and oats
cultivated by the Wards on their various plantations
amounted to millions of pounds, and the vegetables
grown in the gardens were harvested in enormous
amounts. Each year several thousand bushels of corn,
peas, beans, and sweet potatoes were brought from
the large gardens. The Wards also had a salt-making
system on the nearby seashore, which was capable of
producing from thirty to forty bushels of salt per day.

The rector of All Saints Episcopal Church at Pawleys

Island considered the Wards among his most devoted and loyal parishioners, and all other planter families in the parish looked up to the Wards as far as achievement and prestige were concerned. So when word spread that Dr. Allard Flagg was interested in Penelope and Dr. Arthur Flagg considered Georgianna his best friend, no one thought a thing of it. It was a natural course of events.

Alice Flagg was pleased that her brothers had chosen cultured young women of good taste as their friends, and she delighted in the merrymaking that prevailed when the Ward girls came to The Hermitage. But as for Alice, prestige, achievement, culture, and good taste weren't the only qualities to look for when considering someone to marry. And for this, she had someone in mind.

One day a handsome young man came to call on Miss Alice. She had met him when she was shopping one day. Tall Dr. Allard met the man in the flower garden under a huge spreading oak tree and at once came to the conclusion from his speech, manners, profession, and background that the man was not suitable to be a friend of his sister. The caller was sent away without even a word with Miss Alice.

Alice was outraged, and Dr. Allard tried to console her. "Alice," he said, "he is not a professional man. He is a common turpentine dealer. Can't you see that if you choose him as a friend you will be choosing beneath yourself?"

"No!" Alice screamed defiantly. "He has an honorable profession. Don't you recognize the potential of a profession in the pine trees of this region?"

"Yes," Dr. Allard answered. "But in spite of that, the

young man is beneath the notice of a Flagg. Let me hear no more about it!"

But Alice was not to be cowed, and she secretly kept in touch with her friend. After several weeks had passed, she boldly invited him to visit her again at The Hermitage. He agreed to come and told Alice that he would take her for a ride in his buggy, pulled by a team of fine bay horses.

He arrived early in the afternoon and was ushered by a servant into the imposing drawing room of The Hermitage. In a few minutes, Alice descended the staircase in the hallway and hurried into the drawing room. She did not disguise her happiness over seeing her friend. They left the drawing room and went to the wide porch and down the steps, where Alice's beau helped her into his carriage. Just as the suitor was ready to step up into the other side, Dr. Allard appeared on the porch. "Wait!" he cried out.

He ran down the steps, pushed the young man aside, and got into the buggy beside his sister, taking the reins. "I have sent someone to bring my horse," Dr. Allard said. "You'll ride the horse. I'll ride in the carriage with Alice. You may ride beside us and talk to Alice." The young man reluctantly agreed to the arrangement, but there was very little conversation between him and Alice that afternoon as they rode along, he on the horse, she in the carriage with her brother.

Dr. Allard, Dr. Arthur, and their mother had a family meeting, and it was decided that Alice would not be permitted to see her friend again. In the meantime her friend had secretly met her and slipped a ring on her finger and told her to consider it an engagement ring. She was ecstatic. They were very much in love.

When Dr. Allard saw the ring, he demanded that Alice remove it and give it to him so he could return it to the young man. She removed the ring, promising that she would return it, but she slipped it on a ribbon and tied the ribbon around her neck, concealing the ring beneath the collar of her dress.

In another family meeting, it was decided that Alice would be sent to Charleston to attend school so that she would forget about her beau. This was against her wishes, and she went reluctantly, but there was nothing she could do about it.

Alice cried for hours before she unpacked her trunk. She disliked everything she'd ever heard of Charleston: the mansions set far back from the bay, the almost-noble aristocracy, the societies that afforded merriment for the upper class, and most of all, the school where she was now stuck! Tears ran down her cheeks and fell on her dress, the one she treasured above all others, the soft white one with a wide ruffle that served as a collar as well as sleeves, for it draped over her shoulders and arms to her elbows. When she had finished unpacking, she pushed her trunk under the bed. It was only then that she looked around the room that she was to occupy. The bed looked comfortable, but the curtains were of a coarse gauze, and the entire room lacked color. It lacked *warmth*. Everything was so different in Charleston, and she missed her young man so much.

Several weeks passed before Alice began to get accustomed to the city. The pace wasn't quite so leisurely as at Murrells Inlet, and the sounds were startling. There was much screaming and talking when the fishing fleets came in at sunset, some of the fishermen taking care of the sails and cleaning the boats while others prepared the fish for market. Other sounds that surprised Alice were the street cries. Shrimp men chanted "Shrimpy-raw-raw," while vegetable women carried their products in huge baskets balanced on their heads as they called out, "Vejjy-tuble, vejjy-tuble!" Then, there was the rattle of empty milk tins being taken from doorways and full ones left in their places, the ice wagon and the clop, clop of the robust horses that pulled it, and the fire engine's clanging bell as it rushed to a fire. She could hear the chimney sweeps on the roofs and the lamplighters in the evenings. Though Alice did her best to adjust to Charleston and apply herself at school, she did not forget her turpentine dealer back home for one minute. Although he was considered to be "beneath the notice of a Flagg," she loved him with all her heart. Many times a day she pressed a hand to her chest to make sure her ring was still hanging on the ribbon around her neck.

Late one night, after attending a ball at the St. Cecilia Society, Alice became ill. The physician concluded that she was afflicted with malarial fever. Her family must be notified immediately, he told the school authorities.

When word of Alice's illness reached Dr. Allard Flagg, he left The Hermitage at once for Charleston in his carriage. By the time he reached Alice's bedside, she was delirious. Dr. Allard gave her some medication and ordered that her trunk be packed. He was taking her home to The Hermitage.

The journey to Murrells Inlet was not an easy one. It was raining, and the sky was dark with heavy clouds. There were seven rivers to be crossed by ferry, and the roadways were sandy and the edges ill-defined, causing the carriage to slip into a ditch at times. Finally, Dr. Allard arrived between the avenue of oaks leading to The Hermitage. When the frail girl was lifted from the carriage, her brother saw that she was much, much worse.

Alice Flagg drifted into and out of consciousness all night long. Sometime during that first night she was back in her home in Murrells Inlet, she reached for the ring on the ribbon. It was not there! She begged, weakly, "I want my ring. Give me my ring." But her ring was not returned to her. By morning she was dead.

The body of Alice Flagg was dressed in her favorite white dress, and she was buried in the Flagg family plot at All Saints Cemetery near Pawleys Island. A plain marble slab was placed over her grave. Only one word is on the slab — ALICE.

Many times since the death of Alice Flagg there have been accounts of her being seen at The Hermitage. She comes in the front door and moves silently up the staircase to the bedroom that belonged to her. Sometimes she comes early in the evening, and at other times she makes her visits late at night. Also, it is said, she has been seen in the ancient graveyard at All Saints Church. But wherever she is seen, she always seems to be searching for something, while holding her hand over her chest.

Note: Dr. Allard Flagg was a son of Dr. Eben Flagg, and a grandson of Dr. Henry Collins Flagg of Revolutionary War service. Dr. Allard Flagg, his sister Alice, and his brother Dr. Arthur Flagg all had the same middle name — Belin (pronounced Blane). Dr. Arthur Flagg and his wife Georgianna Ward Flagg lost their lives in the terrible storm of October 13, 1893. (See "The Mermaid Storm," *Tales of the South Carolina Low Country,* Winston-Salem, N.C.: John F. Blair, Publisher, 1982.)

The Day the Sheriff
Shot Dr. Buzzard

D O YOU REMEMBER the story about Dr. Buzzard, the Beaufort, South Carolina, witch doctor, escaping from a chained and locked coffin? Well, this tale is about another strange and unexplainable happening in Dr. Buzzard's life. The story was told by his son, Root Man, who is also a practicing witch doctor.

The event took place during the time when the law enforcement officers of Georgetown County were trying their best to prevent Dr. Buzzard from casting spells, invoking and removing hexes, and following other practices involving witchcraft that were causing many people in the Low Country to become almost completely dependent on the witch doctor. After Dr. Buzzard devised a schedule of appointments, sufferers came to him week after week to have hexes or a black root removed, or just to talk about evil spirits at work. Some people had become so dependent on Dr. Buzzard for treatment that they had become ill. Strange noises and weird dreams tormented them, and although nothing seemed to be physically wrong, they lost weight, their hands shook uncontrollably, some went mad, and others died.

The sheriff, together with one of his assistants, decided to have a talk with Dr. Buzzard and try to force him to reduce his power over his patients. They arrived at Dr. Buzzard's house early one morning. Even though it was not yet eight o'clock, several people were on the doctor's porch awaiting their turn to be treated. The sheriff and his assistant waited on the porch until a patient came from inside the house and left. "Okay, Babe, you're next," Dr. Buzzard's voice boomed, and a woman started to go inside the house.

"Wait a cotton-picking minute," the sheriff said gruffly to the woman. "Me and my assistant here are taking your turn today." He opened the screen door and stepped inside, his deputy behind him. They walked down a dark hallway, past the living room and dining room, until they came to a small room in the rear of the house. Dr. Buzzard was sitting on a stool in front of a shelf he called his "altar." On the shelf were a rattlesnake skin, two dead frogs, and several jars containing different colored powders. The air was stale and damp and the light was dim.

"Now looka here," Dr. Buzzard protested, "What you doing here?"

The sheriff looked at Dr. Buzzard, who, as always, was wearing purple sunglasses. "We've come to talk, Buzzard," the sheriff said as he pulled up a chair.

Dr. Buzzard shook his head and looked straight at the sheriff. "Well, talk."

"Now you listen to me," the sheriff began. "Some of these practices of yours is dangerous and has got to stop."

"What for?" Dr. Buzzard rasped. "They ain't hurting you none." His hair stood on end, like quills on a porcupine, as if he had generated within himself a strong charge of electricity.

"You're not a real doctor. You don't give your patients real medicine," the sheriff explained.

"Just lookin' for a quick dollar," the sheriff's assistant, leaning against the wall, murmured.

The sheriff continued. "The people around here won't never stop believing in the power of witchcraft. That's been going on since the first slave ship came over from Africa. It's impossible for me or anybody else to stop them from believing in witchcraft, and I know that as good as you do. But one thing's sure and two are positive. You're treating these people, but you make them come back to you over and over again. And they're not getting well. Some of them's going slap crazy. Now this has got to stop!" The sheriff jabbed a thumb toward the witch doctor. "And I want you to know that just as soon as I can get a good case against you, I'm gonna take you before the Bar of Justice for malpractice."

Dr. Buzzard removed his purple sunglasses and rubbed his eyes. Although his skin was dark, his eyes were blue. He looked straight at the sheriff. "Hear this. I got power like you never even dreamed of. It's plum dangerous for you to be here talking to me like this. Why, if I even used one little bit of my power on you, you'd never sit in the sheriff's office again."

"Show me your power," the sheriff shot back. "I've got power too," he said, patting the thirty-eight caliber pistol in a holster strapped around his waist.

"All right, Sheriff," Dr. Buzzard said. Then he yelled some words in a strange tongue. The woman who had been waiting on the porch ran down the hallway and into the room as if in a trance. Dr. Buzzard didn't say a single word to her, but he fixed her with a stare, and almost immediately she began to beat herself as

20

though she were covered with biting mosquitoes. Foam bubbled from her mouth.

"Stop this!" the sheriff shouted. "Cut it out this minute!" He turned to the woman. "Get back out there on the porch."

As she left the room, she started sobbing.

"Get outta here," Dr. Buzzard said to her. "Go out on the porch and quit that sniffin'. I'll get to you later on, after I finish with the sheriff here."

The sheriff turned to Dr. Buzzard and said, "If you don't stop controlling these people like that, I'm gonna get you if I have to use this." He patted his gun.

"Then use your gun on me," Dr. Buzzard said. "I'd like to see you do it. It won't harm me none."

The sheriff's face turned red with rage. "Let's go outside," he said, pulling his pistol from its holster. He jumped up so quickly the chair he had been sitting in fell to the floor.

"All right," Dr. Buzzard said calmly.

"Remember you asked for this," the sheriff said as he put his pistol back in its holster.

Dr. Buzzard followed the sheriff and his deputy to the porch. The doctor said something to the people waiting there, and then he led the way as the three men walked to the back of the house. When they had reached the rear of the white frame, Dr. Buzzard said, "Now I tell you what we're gonna do. We're gonna have a little test with that gun of yours."

The sheriff stood stiffly, his hand on the butt of the gun in the holster. He appeared a bit wary of Dr. Buzzard.

"I'm going to stand over here on this flat stone," Dr. Buzzard said, "and when I give you the signal, I want you to shoot me."

"You sure about this?" the sheriff asked.

"I never been more sure of anything in my life. I want to show you your gun is worthless against me. Wish I had the newspaper people here to watch this."

"Where do you want me to stand?" the sheriff asked.

"Right here by this tree," Dr. Buzzard said, "but hold it just a minute." The witch doctor took a small bottle from his pocket. He untied a string, which was tied around the bottle, and then removed the top of the container. He poured a few grains of a white, dry mixture into the palm of his hand and then sprinkled it over the spot where the sheriff was to stand. "Now. Stand right there. Right over that spot with the powder on it," Dr. Buzzard said.

The sheriff positioned himself over the spot where Dr. Buzzard had sprinkled the powder. Dr. Buzzard went back to the flat stone and took a stance with his arms folded in front of him.

"Ready?" the sheriff asked.

"Oh, Lord," his assistant wailed. "What if you kill him?" He put a hand over his eyes.

"Shoot!" Dr. Buzzard screamed.

The sheriff moved his feet apart, bent his knees slightly, and drew the pistol, holding it with both hands out in front of him as he took careful aim at the heart of Dr. Buzzard.

"SHOOT!" Dr. Buzzard screamed again.

As the sheriff pulled the trigger for the first shot, his eyes blurred and he could see only a vague figure in front of him. As he squeezed off the second shot, he was stricken with terrible cramps in his stomach, and he bent over in agony. Surely Buzzard must be dead, he thought. And then, as his vision cleared, he saw Dr. Buzzard walking toward him.

"Here's a present for you," Dr. Buzzard said, smiling in triumph.

"What?" the sheriff asked, a bit confused.

"A couple of souvenirs," Dr. Buzzard said, dropping the two bullets in the sheriff's hand.

A Boy Called Light

T HE LITTLE BOY turned the hat over and over in his small, dark hands. "I don't wanna wear no hat. The kids'll laugh at me." He avoided the eyes of his aunt.

"Huggins, you don't have to wear the hat. It's not that important. It was just a small gift. The next time I come to visit your family, I'll try to bring you something that you really like." The boy handed her the hat and started to leave the room. "But, Huggins," she called to him, "why are you so concerned that the children at school will laugh at you?"

"'Cause they laugh at me most all the time," he said, still not looking at her, not turning around.

A frown came to the woman's face. "Can you tell me why they laugh at you?"

"'Cause I told them 'bout the Land's End Light."

She got up, went to a window, folded her arms, and looked at the live oak trees with Spanish moss swinging from the branches. "The Land's End Light. For heaven's sake. There's nothing wrong with telling them about that. I'd think they'd like to hear about that light, awful as it is. That story's been going around for years. Even when I was a child here on Saint Helena Island."

"They even call me Light," the boy said, now looking

24

at his aunt. It was wonderful to have her on his side. "You know, 'cause, shucks, I talked 'bout the Land's End Light." He walked over to the window and stood beside his aunt.

"Well, pay no attention to them," his aunt counseled, turning to face the boy. "If you pay no attention, they'll stop teasing you." She patted the boy's head. "You have a good name. An honorable name. *Huggins Thompson*. Your mama named you for Preacher Huggins. He held a revival on Saint Helena Island the year you were born, nineteen sixty."

The next morning, Huggins waited for the school bus in front of his parents' cabin. It didn't take too long to go to Beaufort when you went on the school bus. But he'd heard his daddy say that when he was a boy, it took all day to go from Saint Helena Island to Beaufort and back. His father left early in the morning, taking feed for his horse, and Uncle Beck ferried him and his horse over the water, back and forth. It was night when his father got back to Saint Helena Island. His daddy didn't go to Beaufort much when he was a boy. He went about two times a year, and one of those times was when his daddy went into town to pay taxes. Now there was a causeway. The ferry was gone. And the school bus could get to Beaufort in about one hour.

The sun glinted on the bus as it came around the curve in the sandy road. This was a typical September day on Saint Helena, hot and glaring with slivers of dust in the air. The bus stopped, the door opened, and Huggins climbed in.

During the morning, the bell rang, and the students left their rooms to go outside for recess. In the hall, a tall white boy called out. "Hey, Light. How come your

25

name's Light when your skin's so dark?" Almost everyone in the hall laughed at Huggins. He hurried out the door.

Huggins thought about it, how they called him Light. What could he do about it? He decided to talk to a friend about it. This friend was the perfect person to talk to because all of the kids at school called him Tree. They called him Tree because he was so tall and skinny, like a pine tree. Huggins liked Tree.

"Don't worry none about it," Tree said. "If them kids didn't call you Light, or me Tree, they'd call us something worse." Huggins thought about that. It was almost the same advice his aunt had given him. He'd try to pay no attention when the kids teased him and called him Light.

A few weeks later the teacher told the children that on the following Tuesday they were going to ride the school bus over to Saint Helena Island, where they would have what she called a "field trip." They would examine some leaves from the different kinds of trees, and they would talk about the birds and the animals that lived on that island, she said.

Tuesday came, and during the afternoon the whole class crowded on the bus and rode across the causeway to Saint Helena Island. Light sat near the back of the bus with Tree. The teacher sat up front, behind the bus driver.

The teacher asked the driver to stop at the salt marsh. Everyone got off the bus, and the teacher explained about the marsh. She told the students that the marsh was an excellent place for a field laboratory. "You can see wildlife in the salt marsh, like the fiddler crabs that roam free as the wind." Then she explained about a great variety of animals that live in the marsh,

26

such as crabs and oysters. "The rise and fall of the tides and the water movements of the marsh determine what animals live in the marsh," she said.

Just before everybody got back on the bus, the teacher told the children to notice the marsh grass. "It is really named Spartina," she said, "and it's not like other grass."

Back on the bus, the teacher told the driver to go to a forest on Land's End Road. It was a dark and gloomy place, but the teacher asked the children to get off the bus again. She explained how this forest had been almost undisturbed by man. The trees she discussed were bald cypress, live oak, scrub oak, longleaf and loblolly pine, and some unusual trees called camphor, tea olive, and toothache trees. Several of the students were amazed to hear that some of the trees were more than one hundred years old. The teacher got carried away in discussing the forest, and it was getting dark when she told everyone to get back on the school bus.

Someone said they would like to see if Land's End Road really went to the end of the land. The teacher thought that would be interesting, and although the road was long, she instructed the driver to take them to the end of it. While riding along, the teacher explained the very unique situation on Saint Helena Island, where there was a wonderful combination of forest, salt marsh, and beaches. Just then the bus came to the end of the road, and it really was the end of the land and the beginning of the ocean.

By now it was dark, and the teacher told the driver to turn the bus around and start back to Beaufort. The children were tired, quiet, some of them slumped in their seats. Just then a brilliant light shone on the bus. The students straightened up alertly and looked

27

around. The light was so strong its heat spread throughout the bus. The driver blinked his eyes as he tried to see ahead and keep the bus on the road.

"What is this?" the teacher asked.

"I don't know," the driver answered.

Some of the girls cried, and the boys were scared too, as scared as if they were seeing a ghost. The white boy who had embarrassed Huggins in the hall at school nervously inquired, "Could this be the light that Light told us about?" Then all the children remembered. "Tell us, Light," the white boy demanded. "Tell us about this light."

"It's the Land's End Light," Huggins said. He wasn't afraid of the light, for he had seen it several times, but the other students were frozen in their seats. The light became even more dazzling and so bright it was as if the sun were beaming right into the bus.

"Is the light going to hurt us?" the white boy asked Huggins. "Is it going to kill us?"

Before Huggins could answer, the bus driver screamed, "Get down! Get down low!" He stopped the bus, and all the students lay down in the seats or in the aisle, some lying on top of others.

"The Land's End Light comes on this road," Huggins said softly, "but it won't hurt you and it won't kill you. It never killed nobody. I know plenty of people who've seen it. Even my daddy saw it when he was a boy."

"What makes it come?" the white boy asked.

"Nobody knows," Huggins answered. "One time Dr. Buzzard made people pay him money, and he took them to see the light. He told them he caused the light. But that wasn't so. There wasn't no truth in that."

"Doesn't Dr. Buzzard have anything to do with the light?" the bus driver called back, unbelieving.

"No," Huggins called to him. "He just took the people's money. Anybody can see the light free. You can see it on this road."

"Hey, Light, you tried to tell us 'bout the Land's End Light before, and we made fun of you and laughed at you," the white boy said. "I'm sorry 'bout that."

"Yeah," a girl sobbed. "I'm sorry too."

And then, just as suddenly as it had appeared, the light went out. It was as dark as pitch. No one could see.

"Now, don't get excited," the teacher said. "Everyone get back in your seats. The light has gone out."

They sat there for a few minutes, and when the driver's eyes had readjusted to the darkness, they were on their way again.

Huggins didn't go all the way back into Beaufort. The bus driver let him off at his house on Saint Helena.

When Huggins got off the bus, the teacher and the bus driver and all the children clapped their hands. The white boy called out, "Thank you, Huggins, for telling us 'bout the Land's End Light."

From that day on, Huggins never did mind when the kids at school called him Light.

Note: Many people in Beaufort, South Carolina, have seen the Land's End Light, and the light can still be seen on the Land's End Road on Saint Helena Island, according to people who live in the vicinity.

The Revival and the Big Shake

B ROTHER SI took charge of the sermon in the little whitewashed church that long ago was an important part of the Edisto landscape but doesn't exist today. He allowed as how happy he was to fill the appointment at the invitation of Sister Hephzibah to "preach the annual." Sister Hephzibah had tried her best to get the people of the Edisto Island congregation to respond in a way that would show their faith in the Lord, but try as she might, she was unable to get the revival going. It was then that she went to Brother Si and asked him to take over and move the people in the congregation toward the Lord. "I ain't conductin' the revival very well," she said to Brother Si. "The revival's conductin' itself."

"Kinda automatic, huh?"

"Zackly!" she said. "I preach the scripture 'bout Job. All 'bout the cattle being down, all the sheeps dyin' and Job's wife, she say, 'You better cuss God and die,' and Job, he hold on; he say to he wife, 'Oh, you speak as a foolish woman. I'll trus' my God 'til me change come.' Oh, I preach Job!" Sister Hephzibah said. "I don't zackly folla the text, but I preach Job!"

"And that didn't shake 'em?" Brother Si asked.

"Not a-tall."

"You got a quartet at church?" Brother Si asked.

"Has us got a quartet!" Sister Hephzibah gushed. "Goldie, she's in the quartet."

"And you still can't get through to 'em?"

"I rassel with that annual," she explained. "I pray. I shout. I clap. I sing the old songs. I 'zaust myself. I can't buckle 'em. They are stiff down. The devil's got 'em. Now *you* try."

"Well, if my foots hold out," Brother Si said, "I'll take the 'pointment and preach the annual."

On August 31, 1886, Brother Si came to the little whitewashed church on Edisto Island. After the quartet sang "Honey in the Rock," he took charge of the sermon and said how happy he was to fill the appointment.

"Now we gonna have a good meetin'," Brother Si began. "God told Abraham he would make great nation," he continued, getting right into his sermon. "God told him, 'Go to seashore. Count them sand! Look up. Count them star!' And Abraham took son, Isaac, to land of Moriah. Son to be offered as sacrifice. Abraham told Isaac, 'Me son, me son. The Lord will provide for you.'"

The congregation echoed, "Will provide!"

Brother Si was glad to hear the response. Perhaps after all he would move the people to express openly their faith in God.

"The time come. Abraham must offer Isaac. Repair to altar. Put him on altar. Tie him hands."

The congregation said in unison, "Take him. Tie him hands."

"Time come," Brother Si continued. "Son must die."

"Must die," the people said.

"Then the angel of the Lord say," Brother Si shouted, "'Don't raise a hand 'ginst that boy! Git ram!'"

The congregation chanted, "Git ram!"

"God moves in mysterious way, him 'bundance to reform," Brother Si said. He looked at the congregation. They were strangely quiet. He had thought that by this time they would be shouting. Usually, when he told the story of Abraham and Isaac, the people in the congregation responded by shouting, and sometimes they went into a frenzy as they identified with Abraham being told by God to offer his only son as a sacrifice. What could he possibly do to add a little heat, Brother Si asked himself. Something to get them red-hot. He decided to talk about heaven. That always flamed up a congregation.

"Heaven be glory," he began. "It's beautiful up there. The streets be lined with gold. There be no rain and cold up there. There be no black and white. All are alike. And when you pass them golden gates, an angel take you and wash you good. Dress you up in fine clothes and put six wings on you. Two on your head, two on your shoulders, two on your foots. Then they teach you to fly. Then the angel come and take you up on Hallelujah Street. Then they take you down Amen Street. And that ain't all 'bout heaven. I just hit the high places."

Brother Si took a deep breath, then went on. "There'll be no rest 'til we reach that home in glory! If you is fateful nuf to get there!" He shook a fist at the congregation, then he went into a song, singing without inviting anyone to join him.

I wants to go to heaven
when I die,
To shout salvation as I fly
I hope I gits there by and by,
To join that number in the sky.

After singing that song, Brother Si prayed the heart-feelingist prayer: "King Jesus! Here's givin' you the blessin' you stored in us. You know we nothin' but lawbreakers 'ginst Thy will. Search each and every heart. If you find anything not planted by your hand lurkin' round the heart, take sword and cut it right to left! Take us and shake us over the brink of eternity." At that moment Brother Si became intensely emotional and shouted, jabbing a fist toward the ceiling of the church. "Gracious God, put fire in our hearts. Let our hearts turn over. Like the eagle stir them nest, stir us up with rich grace from glory. Warn us sinners. Send your lightnin'! Send your thunder! Shake them moss!" The preacher's facial muscles twitched and an arm jerked convulsively, and his black eyes glistened with excitement as he prayed. Sister Hephzibah, in the Amen Corner, waved her turkey-tail fan and patted her feet. "Rattle this island like chains rattlin'. Shake us up, gracious God. Make us fall down and pray."

Just then there was a slight tremor, and the windows in the church rattled.

"Send your warnin', Jesus, and tell us we gotta 'ceive religion like Job had. You 'specks folks to suffer in this world. Ring down on us, Jehovah!"

Another tremor shook the church, and this one was followed by a loud roaring noise. Then four violent shocks came in rapid succession. Shouts arose from the people in the congregation. They left their seats and pushed and squeezed, each one trying to get to the Amen Corner.

"We sinners wouldn't believe," an old man said.

"We're going down Amen Street soon," a woman called out.

"Heaven be glory! It's the tree of life," someone shouted.

Brother Si jumped out a window and ran into the woods. Sister Hephzibah, holding onto her seat in the Amen Corner, watched him make his getaway as the roof of the church gave way. After the frightened people had all gathered around her, she said, "I say this 'bout Brother Si. No preacher ought to pray for what he can't stand up to!"

The people of the congregation went home, and the following day they learned that what they called the "Big Shake," the Charleston earthquake of August 31, 1886, was the most destructive vibration and movement of the earth's surface in the history of the South Carolina Low Country.

Preceded by light tremors, the great shock had come at 9:51 p.m., during Brother Si's fiery sermon. The area disturbed encompassed 2,800,000 square miles, the largest on record. Buildings near the epicenter not completely demolished were wrecked. Property damage exceeded five million dollars and ninety-two people lost their lives. Needless to say, Brother Si never preached again.

The Day Rhett Butler Came
To Hampton Plantation

WILL ALSTON was playing in the yard by the Washington Oak the day important visitors were expected at Hampton Plantation. He was hoping Archibald Rutledge, the owner of the plantation, would come along on his horse and pick him up and go galloping down the avenue of hollies. Will loved to feel the wind flying in his face as he sat in front of the boss. Rutledge often rode up to the Washington Oak in the afternoons and scooped Will up, hardly giving the boy a chance to settle down between his arms before galloping off.

Will realized it wasn't likely that his boss would be out riding his horse that day. Everybody was scurrying about getting ready for the guests. Even his mother didn't have time for him today. She was out in the kitchen cooking a ham for the visitors. Sue Alston had been cooking hams in that kitchen since before the turn of the century. It was no wonder that by the 1930s she really knew how to cook a ham. She boiled it first in a big black pot; then she baked it in the oven, which was located in a wall of the kitchen. The kitchen was a building separate from the big house, and it looked much like the main house. It was constructed of white clapboards, and it even had a pillared veranda. But the kitchen didn't have a big ballroom with a two-story-high ceiling like the main house.

Will glanced toward the ballroom windows, imagining how the visitors would look in their fancy clothes as they danced. At least he supposed they would dance. The people who came from up north always did. When people from the North visited, everybody fussed around to get things ready just like they were doing today. But Sue Alston had told her son that the people expected to arrive were not from up north. They were from Hollywood, California.

But surely, Will thought, even if the people had arrived by late afternoon, the boss would come and tell him when it was quitting time. Rutledge always let Will ring the plantation bell when it was quitting time, and the people working in the cotton would come strolling in, each one carrying a hoe. When Will didn't get to ride the horse with the boss, the highlight of his day was ringing the quitting-time bell.

Just then there was a great flurry of excitement, and someone yelled, "The boat's a-dockin'." All the house servants went to the windows to look toward the South Santee River. Will saw his mother come to the door of the kitchen and look toward the river, then at him. "You be good now. You behave. Them people from Hollywood are a-comin'."

The boy watched as the visitors came walking up the hill to the big house. Some yard helpers were following behind, carrying luggage. A tall man with very black hair and a neatly clipped black mustache walked up to Will. As he spoke, little lights in his eyes did a jig. "How do you do? Do you live here?"

"No, sir," Will answered.

"Where do you live?" the man asked.

"Over yonder, past the Pretty Woods, in a cabin," Will answered. He hoped he was talking correctly because as sure as a possum gets treed, his mother was watching and listening.

The man turned and looked at the white, pillared mansion beyond the Washington Oak. "Beautiful. Just beautiful!" he exclaimed as he turned to Rutledge, who had come out of the house to greet his guests. "Tell me a little of the history of this house," the Hollywood man asked.

Rutledge answered in the soft tone of voice Will had heard him use so often with visitors to the plantation. "The house was built in the 1730s," he said. "But it has been added onto since that time. The wings and veranda were added later on, probably about 1770, when the mistress of Hampton was Harriott Pinckney Horry."

"She must have been quite a mistress," the distinguished man replied.

"She was that, indeed," Rutledge said. "She was the daughter of Eliza Lucas Pinckney, who perfected the cultivation of indigo in this country. Her husband was Charles Pinckney, who was Chief Justice of the Province and Colonial Agent to the Crown.

Will moved closer to the two men so he wouldn't miss anything. The visitor smiled at him before continuing. "I've been told George Washington visited Hampton. Was it during this time?"

"Yes," Rutledge said. He nodded toward the oak tree. "And Washington told Harriott to allow this oak tree to remain right here, even though it interferes with the walkway to the steps leading to the porch. We call it the Washington Oak."

"I'm very impressed."

"Well, come on inside," Rutledge invited. "Let me show you something interesting." He turned to Will. "Come along, boy, since you seem to have made a friend here."

Will felt his cheeks flame at being singled out for special attention, but he was so thrilled to be included that he soon forgot his embarrassment. Nevertheless, he was glad Rutledge went right on talking as they ascended the steps. "You remember the old Swamp Fox, Francis Marion?"

"Yes, I do," the man from Hollywood answered.

"One evening Marion was visiting Harriott here at Hampton," Rutledge continued, "and they were talking about the Revolution. Harriott's husband, Daniel Horry, was away, serving as a captain in the first South Carolina regiment in the Continental Army. Well, as Marion was sitting by the fire in the drawing room, he heard horses' hooves in the avenue. He knew at once that it was his arch enemy, Tarleton. Marion jumped up so fast that he knocked an arm off the ebony Chippendale chair. Harriott directed him to a secret passageway at the rear of the house, and the Swamp Fox made a fast getaway. Come. I'll show you and Will the chair without an arm and the secret passageway."

Will was so excited about getting to see the secret passage that he could hardly believe his ears when, a few minutes later, Rutledge addressed him. "Will, it's quitting time. Want to ring the bell?"

"Yes sir!" Will shouted.

"What bell?" the man from Hollywood asked.

"The plantation bell that we ring for the people in the fields," Rutledge answered. "When they hear the bell, they leave the fields. As Will says, 'It's quittin' time.'" Rutledge winked at Will. "Go ring the bell."

Will ran to the side of the mansion where the huge iron bell was located. Rutledge and his visitor followed to watch.

A wheel, about the height of Will's body, was a part of the bell mechanism. Will placed himself inside the wheel, his legs and arms apart. He pumped himself backward and forward, turning the wheel. His weight, with his feet off the ground, gave just enough leverage to turn the wheel and get the bell in motion. Each time the gong struck the metal bell, it produced a deep, musical sound that reverberated through the woods and cotton fields. A voice from a field in the distance called out, "Quittin' time."

"Well, I'll be!" Will's new friend was excited. "Selznick must see this. This beats anything I've seen on a plantation yet." When Will removed himself from the wheel, the man said, "Will, how would you like to help me while I'm at Hampton? I need a good boy like you to help me carry things around, to help me light the candles in my room."

"Oh, I'd like that, sir," Will replied.

Will soon learned that the crew from Hollywood was visiting Hampton to obtain inspiration for a movie they planned to make. During the following days, Will assisted the man with the black hair and mustache and the eyes that danced a jig. He carried a candelabrum up the stairs each night and put it in the bedroom at the top of the stairway. Each time Will did something for him, the man gave him a dollar.

After staying a few days, the man and his companions left. Will went back to his usual chores, and as the months passed, he almost forgot the tall man from Hollywood.

In 1939 a woman who lived on an adjoining planta-

39

tion came to see Sue Alston and her son. She asked Will if he knew what a motion picture was. When Will said he didn't know, the woman asked Sue if she could take him to Charleston to view a motion picture, and Sue gave her consent.

Will went to Charleston with his neighbor, and he sat beside her in the theater. The picture was *Gone With the Wind*. In the opening scenes, a boy just like Will ran to a plantation bell, put himself into the wheel, and rang the bell. Just like at Hampton, a voice from the fields cried, "Quittin' time."

"Is that me?" Will asked, almost shouting.

"Please, you are supposed to talk quietly in a theater," the woman admonished Will. "No, that is not you, but it looks just like you, and that boy rang the plantation bell just as you do. Remember when a crew of people from Hollywood came to Hampton? They saw you ring the bell. Will, I think if they hadn't seen the way you ring the bell, this scene wouldn't be in the picture."

Will sat quietly as the picture on the screen continued. "Look! It's him!" In his excitement, Will forgot he was supposed to whisper. It was his old friend, the man from Hollywood who had given him the dollars and had been so kind to him.

In the motion picture, they called him Rhett Butler.

Note: On September 15, 1973, Archibald Rutledge's funeral was held on the porch of Hampton. Before Rutledge's death, he deeded Hampton to the State of South Carolina, and he insisted that it be stipulated in the deed that Will Alston have employment at Hampton for the remainder of his life. Visitors to Hampton today may meet Will Alston, who tells the old plantation stories with pride.

Hampton Plantation is now a state park. Hampton Plantation State Park is located near US 17, thirty miles north of Charleston, six miles north of McClellanville. Take Secondary Road 10-857, and continue to the gate.

The Lizard in the Medicine Chest

OLD MAN OBIE HINES had a problem: there was something in his nose. He couldn't breathe very well, and he was near 'bout crazy from frustration. His family was so worried about him that they finally sent him to Aunt Liza, a root doctor. If Aunt Liza couldn't cure Old Man Obie, nobody could, they figured.

Aunt Liza made her own medicine, using for ingredients those things that had been gathered from the woods and fields. In other words, the woods and fields comprised her medicine chest. She made a bitter tea from weeds which caused profuse perspiration, and she had a concoction that proved effective in curing fever. She mixed an iron tonic after gathering cinders from a blacksmith's shop, pounding them into a fine powder and stirring in enough molasses and ginger to make the mixture taste good.

But Aunt Liza's specialty was her collection of little bags of roots. She cultivated certain plants for the purpose of tying their roots in bags, and she called the bags "asphetite bags." She tied in the bags what she called black snake root and Sampson snake root. Aunt Liza had dozens of asphetite bags tied around her neck and sewn into the seams of her full, floor-length skirts. Sometimes all it took to cure an illness was one wave of Aunt Liza's skirts.

42

If Aunt Liza's cures with root medicine were not successful, she resorted to other methods to effect a cure. It was a known fact that she sometimes collected small animals and insects in the fields and used them in unusual ways in order to cure a patient who was ill.

The day Old Man Obie called on Aunt Liza, she was in fine form for a root doctor. Her eyes were cocked, her face wrinkled, her nose crinkled, and when she talked, her face worked convulsively. She hadn't a tooth in her head, and her gums were blue. Besides that, her head was shaped funny.

"What's the trouble?" Aunt Liza asked old Man Obie.

"I'm near 'bout crazy with something in my nostril," he replied. "I can't clear my nostril and I feel addled."

Aunt Liza first had Old Man Obie blow his nose. He blew, but that didn't help him. She asked him to try to sneeze, but he couldn't bring on a sneeze.

Aunt Liza gave Old Man Obie some of her root medicine and told him to go back to his cabin, stay in bed for two days, and let her know if he improved.

Two days later, Old Man Obie was back at Aunt Liza's shack. "Something's still in my nostril," he said. "I just know I can't last the week out if something's not done."

Aunt Liza waved her asphetite bags at the man and told him to go home and wait for a couple of days and see what happened. After two days, Old Man Obie came back to see Aunt Liza. "Something's still in my nostril," he said. "If you can't do something for me, I'll have to go to another witch doctor."

Aunt Liza began to think about the ailment and wondered if it was physical or mental. She knew how to treat both. With a slight wave of her skirts, she left the cabin and went into a nearby field. After awhile she returned, and it seemed that she was concealing something in a pocket of one of her skirts.

"Close your eyes," she said to Obie.

He closed his eyes.

Aunt Liza reached deep into a pocket of her skirts, and when she took her hand from the pocket, with her other hand she threw a rag over it. Her hand, under the rag, was shaking so much she could barely keep the rag in the right place.

"Now, Obie," Aunt Liza said, "keep your eyes closed, but when I say blow, I want you to blow your nose just like you're blowing a horn trying to round up all the people in the fields."

Old Man Obie nodded, but he didn't open his eyes.

"You know that field over on the Pee Dee?" she asked.

"You mean that field of more'n two hundred acres?"

"Yes," she said. "Well, when I say blow, I want you to blow your nose like you're trying to make the people over there in that field hear you." Aunt Liza held the rag over her hand and said, "BLOW!"

Old Man Obie blew so hard the blood vessels in his face stood out.

Aunt Liza pulled from under the rag a slick, black lizard. "See this?"

Obie's eyes got as big as cabbages. His mouth opened, but no words came out.

Holding the lizard by the head and the tail, Aunt Liza said, "This was in your nose. But it's out now. Go on home. You'll be all right from now on."

Old Man Obie was breathing through his nose just fine when he left Aunt Liza and he never had any trouble with his nose again.

The Girl Who Was Buried Alive

W HEN THEY WERE youngsters, Marion Whaley pushed his brother Maynard into the old marble mausoleum that stands in the burying ground at the rear of Edisto Presbyterian Church. It was a scary thing to do, for in July 1850 a young girl who was visiting Edisto Island died with diphtheria and was buried in the mausoleum. Later on, it was learned that she had been *buried alive*.

"It was me or him," Marion Whaley explained years later, "Maynard planned to push me into the mausoleum where the girl had been buried alive, and he was going to prop up the marble door in the entrance opening so there could be no escape. I would have had to stay there overnight. When I learned of the prank he planned to play on me, I just beat him to it. I shoved him inside the vault and pushed the marble door into place, and the door remained shut until I came back the next morning and freed him."

That part of Edisto Island is as gloomy today as it must have been in 1850. Huge oaks, with pendulous masses of Spanish moss looping from limb to limb hover over the land, and strange things happen there. Once a white stallion jumped high into the air and died when he was caught in the fork of an oak tree. The skeleton of the animal remained in the tree long

45

after every bit of the flesh had been consumed by birds and animals, and for years people came to view the horse bones in the old oak tree.

The Edisto Presbyterian Church was designed by James Curtis, a Charleston architect, and was built in the early 1830s. It looks today much as it did then. A weathervane adorns the steeple. Interior walls are of heart pine paneling. The pews have entrance gates, some of them retaining the original hinges. Those who look up can see the wood benches once used by slaves. Generation after generation of Edisto Islanders have knelt in worship at the rail that encloses the chancel of the white clapboard church.

The graveyard that surrounds the church on three sides dates back to the eighteenth century, and the names on the grave markers are evidence of prominent South Carolina families who have been buried there, many having died of diphtheria. The names include Edings, Mikell, Seabrook, LaRoche, Hopkinson, and Whaley.

Diphtheria was a common disease in the South Carolina Low Country during the 1800s. The first effective diphtheria antitoxin was not developed until 1890. This contagious disease spread throughout the barrier islands of South Carolina in 1850, and when the telltale yellowish-gray patch appeared on the throat of the young girl who was buried alive, it wasn't long before she went into a coma so deep that word mistakenly came from the physician that she had died.

As there was no artificial preservation of dead bodies on Edisto Island before the Civil War, it was the practice to bury the dead as soon as possible after their demise. So word was sent to neighboring plantations that the girl's funeral would be held that very afternoon. As the people of Edisto Island prepared to attend the funeral and burial of the girl who had been visiting in the home of a planter family, loving hands prepared her body and dressed her in the pink dress that had been her favorite.

After the funeral was held in the sanctuary, the body was placed in a marble mausoleum behind the church, under a canopy of oaks and pines. The tomb door was a broad, flat, thick piece of marble, hinged on one side. It was closed and locked.

In the amber glaze of the afternoon, the mourners left the cemetery, walking among the marble forms of cherubs, urns, and other symbols of eternal sleep among the trees. Just before leaving the burial ground, some turned for a last look at the mausoleum with the family name, J. B. Legare, carved above the door. The sepulcher lacked columns, but it could have doubled for a tiny Greek temple.

Some fifteen years later, one of the men of the Legare family was killed in an accident. His body was prepared for burial and taken to the church, where his funeral was held. When the heavy door to the family mausoleum was opened so that the remains of his body could be interred, there, to the horror of the members of the family, was the skeletal frame of the young girl who had been buried earlier. From the position of her remains, it was clear that she had been buried alive, and at the time of her death she had been trying to escape from the mausoleum. Members of the family felt the horror the young girl must have felt when she realized she was trapped, and they felt the panic that must have driven her to try — without hope — to escape.

The man was entombed, as were the skeletal remains of the young girl, and it was several weeks before any of the family returned to the mausoleum. When they did, they found the door to the vault standing open. The door was closed again and fastened in such a way that it seemed impossible that it could ever be opened again. However, strangely, in a few weeks an elder of the church discovered the door standing open again.

Word spread throughout the area that the spirit of the young girl who had been buried alive would not allow the door to remain closed so that no one else would be buried in the tomb alive. For more than a hundred years it was impossible to keep the door to the mausoleum closed.

About thirty years ago the door was again attached in such a way that it was concluded it would be impossible for it to be opened except with certain heavy equipment. But a few days later, the door was found not only open but removed from the mausoleum at the hinges. The concerned administrators of the church then had the door reinstalled and fastened by a heavy iron chain. But within a few days the door was again lying on the ground in front of the mausoleum!

Today vines grow in the cracks of the marble mausoleum, and spider webs and wasp nests festoon the doorframe. And the stubborn marble door lies broken into three pieces on the ground at the vault entrance.

The Ghost in the Attic

T HE YEAR WAS 1910, and the Henson family had just moved into the farmhouse they were renting from Mrs. Bonnet on the outskirts of a small village not far from Charleston. One night, as Mr. Henson, his wife, two sons, and one of his daughters were in the parlor gathered around a fire blazing on the hearth, his fourteen-year-old daughter came into the room shrieking with terror. Mr. and Mrs. Henson both jumped up at the same time, frightened but curious, and went to her.

"It's the ghost," Ella said in a trembling voice. "It's the Bonnet ghost." Ella was still holding a piece of linen on which she had been embroidering colorful flowers, and she was pulling at the cloth abstractedly.

By now, Mary Bell, who was seven, was also crying. She was especially scared of ghosts, no doubt as a result of tales her older brothers had told her. "Did you see the Bonnet ghost, Ella?" she asked her sister.

"No, but I heard it," Ella said. "He was dragging something across the attic floor."

"Oh, I can't stand it," Mary Bell wailed, her black curls jouncing as she shook her head. She covered her brown eyes with her hands.

"What are we going to do?" cried the brown-haired, blue-eyed Ella.

Mrs. Henson calmed the girls, then she turned to her husband and admitted quietly that she too had heard noises from the attic. Mr. Henson decided it might be a good idea to talk about the ghost. "Let's bring the subject right out in the open and talk about it," he suggested.

The girls' oldest brother, Charlie, was the first to speak up. He told his family he had heard all about the Bonnet ghost even before they had moved into the house. He had been told that a ghost dragged a heavy object across the attic floor each night. The ghost was supposedly that of Mr. Luke Bonnet, a banker who had shot himself after it was reported that he had embezzled some of the bank's funds.

"And who told you this?" his father asked.

"The people at the general store in the village are all talking about the Bonnet ghost," Charlie explained. "All you have to do is go in there and pretty soon you'll hear talk of it."

Mrs. Henson wanted to know who had told the girls about the ghost. Charlie sheepishly admitted that he and his brother Walter had told them "a bit" about the ghost.

"And just what *did* you tell the girls?" his mother questioned.

"Only that the Bonnet ghost drags something from one part of the attic to another," Charlie hastened to explain, sensing that he was about to get into trouble. "No one knows exactly what it is that the ghost drags around, but it sounds like a heavy metal box."

"That's what he just did," Ella affirmed, frightened all over again as she got caught up in her brother's explanation. "I heard him drag the metal box!"

"I did too," Mary Bell chimed in, her voice high-pitched and her eyes wide.

Everybody looked at Mary Bell, unconvinced that she had heard the ghost. Mary Bell often took sides with her sister. Her father decided not to press the child, who was near hysterics, by asking questions. Besides, he at least was sure that no ghost existed. Some of his family had just fallen victim to the ghost stories.

He turned to his sons. "Charlie, go to the attic and investigate. Walter, you go with Charlie. When the two of you find there is no ghost there, it might soothe the fears of your sisters."

"Why do I have to go?" asked Walter, who seemed uninterested and, like his father, totally unconvinced that any ghost existed.

"Two heads are better than one in something like this!" his father replied. "You don't need a better reason than that."

While Charlie and Walter were taking down the board from the closet ceiling and climbing up into the attic, their father talked to Ella and Mary Bell. Being a religious man, he tried to impart to his daughters the courage he found in his faith in God. "You must not fear anything or anyone," he said. "Only fear God."

When the boys came back, they said they had seen nothing to suggest that a ghost had been dragging a metal box in the attic. "But," Charlie added, "that is not to say I don't believe that the Bonnet ghost lives in the attic. In that respect, I'm with Ella and Mary Bell."

"You just believe that crazy talk down at the store," Walter mumbled.

"Well, if anyone in town talks about the ghost, don't

discuss it with them," Mr. Henson advised his family. "That goes for all of you." Then he turned to Ella and Mary Bell. "And don't you girls listen to any more talk of ghosts. There is *no ghost* in this house!"

About a week later, the family was again sitting around the fire when they heard a dragging sound above. Instantly they became still, listening. It sounded exactly as if something heavy was being moved across the attic floor from one side to the other.

With a determined look on his face, Mr. Henson got up, went into the bedroom closet, removed several boards from the closet ceiling, and pulled himself up into the attic with the help of his two sons. The mother and the two girls sat quietly in the parlor. They listened to each of Mr. Henson's steps as he walked around in the attic. When he returned to the living room, he said that he had examined the attic thoroughly and had found no ghost there.

"Listen, I hear it again!" Mary Bell screeched. "I hear it now."

The others heard nothing and looked at Mary Bell skeptically. Her mother quickly took the child from the room and put her to bed.

The next night they all heard the sound again. Something was definitely being moved from one side of the attic to the other! When the sound stopped, the house became quiet, very quiet.

Mary Bell broke the silence. "There is a ghost up there. Mama said so."

Mr. Henson looked sharply at his wife.

"See?" Ella said, pointing a finger at her little sister. "I told you not to say that. Now you've upset papa."

"There *is* a ghost up there, and I know it," Mary Bell cried.

52

Two days later Mr. Henson went into the small town to find out for himself what was being said about the ghost. He knew he had to get to the bottom of this matter if his family was ever going to calm down. He went first to the general store.

The people in the store reported that word had spread all over the village that Mr. Bonnet's ghost was indeed residing in the attic of the house. They were all too willing to repeat the whole story. Mr. Bonnet had worked at the bank in town and had been accused of embezzlement. Soon afterwards, his wife confessed to the bank authorities that her husband had indeed embezzled some money. She revealed that her husband was keeping the funds in the attic of their house in a heavy, metal box. He had brought the money from the bank by concealing it in the socks he wore, she explained. She went on to say that being the honest person she was, she felt it her duty to expose her husband and return the money, painful as it was for her to do so. This led to his suicide.

As the story going around town revealed, just before Mr. Bonnet took his life, he told his wife that she would never again enjoy living in their home. Apparently, Mrs. Bonnet told this in confidence to a servant. When her servant broke the confidence and told the story to a friend, it wasn't long before nearly everyone in the town was talking about it. Poor Mrs. Bonnet was forced to leave the house and make her home with a sister after her husband's ghost started dragging the heavy object across the attic floor every night.

Many people in town sympathized with Mrs. Bonnet. Always quiet and conscientious, she was now exposed to terrible gossip. And she had helped the people at the bank so much. Because a change in the bookkeeping system was taking place at that time, no one at the bank could figure out just how much money was missing. Mrs. Bonnet not only explained how her husband had brought the money home in his socks, she also told them how much money he stole, returning to them the entire amount, three thousand dollars.

After he heard the whole sad tale, Mr. Henson then went to the bank and talked with a man who told him the same story he had heard at the general store. He went to see the funeral director, who had taken care of Mr. Bonnet's remains and who was a friend of Mrs. Bonnet's. He, too, substantiated the story.

"We will not let this silly superstition get the best of us," the father told his family after his return from town. "We will live here, pay Mrs. Bonnet her monthly rent, which she surely needs now that her husband has gone to his reward, and we will be close-mouthed when someone speaks to us of the ghost. We will in no way become a part of the gossip, a part of this tale." But even as he was talking, the sound in the attic began, and Ella and Mary Bell both started to weep.

Mr. Henson still stubbornly refused to acknowledge that a ghost might live in his attic. He decided to go and see Mrs. Bonnet. The monthly rent would soon be due. He would take the money to her and use that as an excuse for the visit. And while he was there, he reasoned, he might just drop a hint that if the dragging sound continued night after night, the family might be forced to move. He didn't know what Mrs. Bonnet could do about the sound, but it was worth a try. After all, if the sound kept up and the stories of the ghost persisted, it would surely affect his children, especially Mary Bell, in some permanent way.

The next day he visited Mrs. Bonnet at her sister's house. Although she was only forty, she looked sixty. She told Mr. Henson that it would not disturb her in the least to speak of her husband. And to his astonishment, she spoke quite openly about her husband's ghost.

"My husband told me before he killed himself that I would never be happy in the house again, and that I would never receive any pleasure as long as I lived there. I didn't know what he meant at the time," she continued, speaking softly, now and then dabbing her eyes with a lace handkerchief. "But it was true. I wasn't happy in that house after his death, so I came here to live with my sister."

"I have two daughters," Mr. Henson said, "and although they are unharmed, they are somewhat the worse for wear because of the harassment of your husband's ghost." He suddenly realized that, for the very first time, he had acknowledged that he believed there was a ghost in the house. "We hear the dragging sound night after night, and when I investigate, there is nothing in the attic that could possibly have produced the sound."

"But why have you come to me?" Mrs. Bonnet asked, continuing to talk without giving the man an opportunity to answer. "I, too, am at an utter loss to understand my husband's motives." With her hands in her lap, she twisted her handkerchief. "This is a difficult and sad time for me. The hours pass very slowly."

Just then a pallor spread over Mrs. Bonnet's face, and she gave a tiny cry of grief. Then she continued, "The bank is a private bank, and my husband told me he was afraid he would mismanage it and lose his depositors' money. You see, my husband was never very good at figures. Oh, he knew how to run his bank when it was small, but as it grew, he didn't quite understand how to match the bookkeeping system with the bank's growth. He was worried that something would happen to his depositors' money. Most of them were his good friends."

Mrs. Bonnet stopped talking for a moment and took a deep breath. Mr. Henson thought she looked weaker than just moments before, and he wondered if her mind was wandering. He also started to wonder if she was speaking the truth.

"I was always good at figures," Mrs. Bonnet continued. "So I thought I would help my husband. I asked him to bring the bank's ledgers home so I could explain to him the bookkeeping system. He didn't want anyone at the bank to know that he was bringing the ledgers home and that I was the one who was going over them. I had him carry the ledgers in a paper bag, and he suggested bringing home some money as well. It would be much easier for me to explain it all to him, he thought, when I had some cash with which to illustrate the system. It made sense for him to carry the cash in his socks. Then, if the ledgers were somehow discovered in the paper bag, the cash wouldn't be found with them." She looked away and gave a little sob. "I cautioned him to tell his employees that he was commencing a new bookkeeping system, just in case one of them discovered that the ledgers were taken from the bank overnight."

She dabbed at her eyes with the handkerchief before going on. "I'll be frank with you. He had learned a great deal, and we were just about to discontinue the practice of bringing the ledgers and cash home when it was discovered that some money was missing. As you know, I helped the people at the bank by returning the three thousand dollars that my husband had hidden in the attic."

"I must be frank with you as well," the father said, having had enough of both Mrs. Bonnet and her husband's ghost. "I have decided that this will be the last rent money I will pay you, for I feel it is necessary for us to move away at the end of the month." He left quickly, after handing the last rent money to Mrs. Bonnet.

Not quite two weeks had passed when Charlie astonished his father at supper with the news that Mrs. Bonnet had died the previous day.

"Died?" his father asked uncomprehendingly.

"Yes," Charlie went on quickly. "Her sister was cleaning her room after the body was taken away, and none of you will ever guess what she found!" They were all sitting on the edge of their seats now. "She found a Bonnet Bank strong box under Mrs. Bonnet's bed, and it had nearly twenty thousand dollars in it!"

The family decided to continue living in the Bonnet house, but they never forgot the Bonnet ghost, even though after Mrs. Bonnet's death, the dragging sound in the attic was never heard again.

The Witches' Spell

MANY PEOPLE BELIEVE there are more witches in the world today than at any other time. Whether or not this is true is uncertain, but there are two well-known witches on the coast of South Carolina near Charleston who say they are actively casting spells. Not long ago a man who conducts a weekly radio talk show in Charleston invited the witches to be his guests.

Just before time to go on the air, in an effort to lessen the tension and relax his guests, the talk show host asked the witches to explain to him the casting of spells.

"Well, we have all kinds of spells," the red-haired girl named Jessica said. She was dressed in a fashionable suit, and her hair was newly coiffured.

"Could you cast a spell on me?" the host asked, not too serious about the whole thing.

"Of course," the other witch said. She had long black hair and wore a white dress that was accented with a red, white, and blue pin in the shape of a flag. Her name was Tiffany.

"What kind of spell could you cast on me?" the man asked, still endeavoring to warm up his guests before air time.

"Well," Jessica said, "we have one that will bring you money."

"Money!" the host exclaimed, becoming more interested. "How much money would the spell bring to me?"

"As much as you need," Tiffany answered, as she smoothed her skirt and crossed her long, slim legs.

"Well, I need money for so many things," the host said, rubbing his palms together. "For example, I need money for a new furnace before winter sets in."

"Does it get that cold in Charleston?" Jessica asked. "We haven't been here too long and haven't lived here during the winter."

"We have some cold weather all right," the host said. "Oh, there are balmy days all through the winter, but then again, we have some cold spells." He looked at his watch. "Yep, we have some cold weather, and I sure need a new furnace. A heat pump is the kind I'd really like to have."

Tiffany looked at Jessica. "Let's put the spell on him to get him the money for the new furnace!"

"Yes," Jessica said, her eyes twinkling in amusement. "Let's do it."

"Wait a minute," the host said. "I'm not so sure. If you brought me some money from a spell, it might be, uh, what you might call bad money, you know?"

"We have other spells," Tiffany said.

"What other spells do you have?"

"We could put a relaxing spell on you. Make you relax more."

"Hey! I think that's the spell for me. My work here at the studio keeps me tense. It's pretty stressful."

Jessica held a hand before her and pondered her nails. They were long and tapered, a brilliant red, and perfectly manicured. "The thing about that spell is, well, if we put the spell on you and you relax too much, we might be going to your funeral."

"Heavens! I don't want that spell. Let's go back to money." The host again looked at his watch. Just then a red light above his desk blinked on and off. "Hey. It's almost air time. We'll talk about it later."

An ON THE AIR sign lighted up. A red light above the door flashed on, then off, then back on. It kept flashing on and off.

The host cleared his throat, nodded to his guests, and began to speak into the microphone. "Today I have as my guests, two witches." He looked at them appraisingly, then continued. "You wouldn't really know to look at them that they are witches. They are fashionably dressed, even what you might call chic, and they are witty and intelligent. I've just been talking to them before air time and, folks, believe me, you'd never know these girls are witches. Now, let's meet them. They are Jessica and Tiffany."

The host talked to the witches for the thirty minutes that the program was on the air. He didn't ask them any questions that would divulge their secrets of casting spells, but he led them through the conversation as they explained that they had been born in Virginia and had lived on the coast of North Carolina and had moved to Charleston only a few weeks before.

Jessica explained that in earlier years many people believed a witch could be either a man or a woman who was supposed to have supernatural power, but people no longer believe in male witches. There are, however, some men called wizards, or warlocks, who are thought to have supernatural abilities.

60

Tiffany said that the oldtime belief that witches can ride through the air on a broom isn't true. Both girls laughed, and Tiffany continued to say that, oh yes, the brooms were supposed to fly anywhere, at any desired speed, and at any height, but that she and Jessica had never ridden on a broom.

The host concluded the conversation by telling his listeners that Jessica and Tiffany were indeed bewitching. While still on the air, he thanked the girls for being on the show, and then he told his audience who his guest would be on the next show. He pushed a button, which turned off the microphone.

"Now," he said, "let's get back to that spell. Are you serious? Can you get me some money?"

Tiffany, now very animated and at ease, laughed and said, "We are dead serious. Sure. We'll put the spell on you, and you'll get the money for your new furnace."

The host leaned backed in his swivel chair. "Then put it on me."

Tiffany reached for her purse.

The man closed his eyes, then opened one. "You won't condemn me if I'm a bit skeptical, will you?"

"You won't be a believer until you receive the money," Tiffany answered. "After the spell takes effect, you won't be skeptical anymore." She took from her purse a small, red plastic case and zippered it open, removing a pair of fingernail scissors. She walked over to the host, and Jessica joined her. Tiffany lifted one of the man's hands. "You don't mind if I clip a nail, I hope." She cut a sliver of his thumbnail and handed it to Jessica. Tiffany then clipped a few strands of hair that were hanging over the man's forehead.

61

"Now we have the ingredients for the spell," she said. She handed the lock of hair to Jessica. "Do you feel any supernatural forces yet?" she asked the host.

"Not the remotest," he said emphatically.

"Well, you could relax a little," Jessica suggested.

"When my mind and body have been taken over by evil forces, let me know," the host wisecracked.

"Let's begin the ritual," Jessica said. She then dropped on the carpet in front of the host the piece of fingernail and lock of hair. The girls stood side-by-side, looking down at the ingredients on the carpet.

After a moment Jessica said, "The forces are swirling now."

"I know," Tiffany answered.

"If I go berserk, restrain me," the host joked.

The witches didn't respond, but they talked to each other in subdued voices, speaking in a strange tongue. After about five minutes had passed, Jessica said, "It is done."

"You will receive the money after seven days, but before twelve days," Tiffany explained.

The witches picked up their purses and left the studio.

Ten days later the host received an unexpected check. It was for $2,400. The check came from a former employer who had suddenly decided to reimburse the money the host had paid into a profit-sharing plan during his term of employment. The following day another check came. This one was in the amount of $600, and it was a refund on an insurance policy for which the host had overpaid. Within days, the man had a heat pump installed in his home.

Three weeks after that, the host had to go to Dallas

on a business trip. He flew to Charlotte, where he boarded a flight for Dallas/Fort Worth. During the flight, the passengers were served a light snack, and it was while the host was eating a sandwich that he began chatting with the man sitting next to him. The talk got around to the occupation of the host, and he explained his job and told his seatmate about the witches and the spell they had cast on him.

"And did the money come to you?" the man asked the host.

"Oh, yes. Just as the witches said it would."

"And did you spend the money?"

"Of course," the host said. "I bought the heat pump I had wanted for a long time."

"You never should have spent the money," the man said to the host.

"Why?"

"Because it was bad money. Something quite dreadful might happen to you as a result of using the money the witches got for you."

"Like what?"

"I don't know what the spirits will do for retribution, but I'll tell you this. I've done some research on the supernatural, and I can tell you that you never should have used the money." He looked out the window at the snowy clouds beneath the plane.

"Is there anything I can do to rectify using the money?" the host asked nervously. "Anything that would counteract my using the money?"

"Not that I know of," the man answered, still looking out at the clouds.

The plane landed, and the men walked together to the baggage pickup area. It was after the host had taken his baggage that he heard himself being paged over the public address system. He was asked to go to the ticket counter.

"You have a call," an airline employee said, pushing a phone toward him. "Line three."

"You must come home at once," the next-door neighbor of the host said.

"Why?"

"Your house has burned."

"Oh, no," the host moaned. "Did it burn completely?"

"Yes. I'm sorry."

"Was everything destroyed? My coin collection? And the things that belonged to my mother?" He was pale and trembling.

"Everything is gone," the neighbor said. "There is nothing left but a mound of ashes."

"Do you know what caused the fire?" the host asked.

"The fire marshal and a team of investigators are still there," the neighbor answered. "They have worked so hard. I went out and got boxes of fried chicken to bring to them. While they were eating, I overheard the fire marshal say he believes the fire started as a result of faulty wiring in your new heat pump."

Plantation for an Old Maid

D ANIEL HORRY first married a woman named Judith, and they lived at beautiful Hampton Plantation on the South Santee River, north of Charleston and south of Georgetown. When Judith died, Daniel was considered to be the most eligible man in the South Carolina Low Country. Harriott Pinckney was the girl he chose to be his second wife. At first, after their marriage, everything for Harriott and Daniel went well.

Harriott brought to her marriage nearly perfect credentials for being the mistress of Hampton. She was a daughter of Eliza and Charles Pinckney, a brilliant couple, popular both in South Carolina and in England. Harriott entertained the top ranks of society at Hampton and also at Daniel's town house in Charles Town. One could say that Harriott brought to the South Carolina Low Country attention like that received by Jacqueline Kennedy while she was First Lady. Harriott's first child, Daniel Huger Horry, was born in August 1769, and a daughter, Harriott Pinckney Horry, was born in 1771.

Shortly after the Boston Tea Party in 1773, Harriott's husband was appointed to head a committee of patriots in Charles Town. In a show of support for the Boston rebels, the committee made arrangements for supplies to be accepted at the port of Charles Town during the time the Boston port was closed by Britain as punishment for the Tea Party.

Daniel played an important part in the politics of the colonies. He was a rice planter, and political power fell into the hands of the planters. When the Americans openly declared themselves in revolution against British rule, Daniel Horry was elected captain in the first South Carolina regiment in the Continental Army. Harriott still entertained lavishly, and her reputation as a hostess as well as the beautiful mistress of Hampton spread throughout the colonies. Harriott invited friends to Hampton to dine at sumptuous buffets and to dance. Among those she entertained at Hampton were General Francis Marion and George Washington.

Even with all of her social obligations, Harriott never failed to oversee her children's education. Books in the Hampton library included Sir Edward Cooke's *Laws of England*, printed in 1590. French classics of the eighteenth century were also on the shelves, as well as a collection of sermons. There were works of Montesquieu, Corneille, Racine, and Voltaire. An elegant edition of Shakespeare was in the library. When Harriott decided that her son's education must reach beyond that which he could achieve in South Carolina, she wrote to General Nathanael Greene, an American who was famous for his campaigns against the British in South Carolina, and asked permission to send her son to England to be educated and to send along enough Santee River rice to pay for the education. Not only was she given permission to send her son to England, but her husband was dispatched to accompany the boy across the Atlantic.

With her son in England, being educated and conditioned to his circumstances as the future owner of Hampton and as a rice planter, Harriott began to worry about her daughter, also named Harriott. Harriott the younger was anything but pretty. She had a coarse face, without a noticeable jawline or cheekbones, and the skin on her face was adorned with pimples and warts. But Harriott the elder never slacked in her ambition for her daughter and introduced her to and instructed her in the social graces.

Eventually the war was over, and it was thought that the family could again be together. But Daniel died of bilious fever on November 12, 1785, at Hampton. After the death of her husband, and with the privations of war ending, Harriott decided to enlarge Hampton House. She included young Harriott in all of the plans in an effort to perk her up. The entrance, located on the Santee River side of the mansion, was moved to the inland side, and matching wings were added on either side of the house. The west wing consisted of a great master bedroom with ceilings two stories high, and the east wing was a ballroom forty-two feet long, with a twenty-eight-foot-high arched ceiling. Floorboards in the ballroom were all of one length and were believed to be the longest floorboards in America. The walls had cypress panels, and Delft tiles outlined the seven-foot-wide fireplace. The lovely tiles pictured Biblical characters such as David and Goliath and the Good Samaritan, as well as wildflowers, trees, and seascapes.

European furniture, paintings, silver, and china were sent to the mansion from friends and relatives who lived in England and France. There were tables arriving, it seemed, on each boat that came to Charleston. There were marble-top tables, tables of rosewood and Santo Domingo mahogany, tables for every conceivable use.

To Harriott's absolute delight, her son Daniel married a niece of the Marquis de Lafayette, and he and his bride traveled to France. But her daughter, now twenty-six, would probably never marry. Most self-respecting girls of that day had been married long before they reached the age of twenty-six! Harriott decided that she must do something to give her daughter a lifelong interest. Then an idea came to her. She would build for her daughter a fine house on a nearby tract of acreage. If she owned her very own plantation, the young Harriott would surely take more of an interest in her appearance and companionability.

The site of the new plantation was adjacent to The Wedge. The Wedge Plantation was noted for its beautiful gardens, and it was also famous as the plantation that had been built by William Lucas, a son of the Englishman who had invented and built the first American rice mill. Harriott told her daughter that she had bought the large tract of land and planned to construct a manor house that would be noted even in England for its beauty. The young Harriott was elated. She pictured herself as the mistress of her very own plantation, one on which no amount of money would be spared. This reaction pleased her mother very much. The plan was working!

The new manor house was built, and the talk throughout the South was of the young, single woman who would be its mistress. There was much speculation as to whether she would be the striking hostess that her mother was at Hampton.

The mother didn't stop with just building the house. She ordered bulbs from Holland and hired a man to arrange the features of the landscape. Extensive gardens were planted.

Finally, it was time for the young Harriott to move into her new house. The year was 1797, and the plantation had a name: Harrietta.

Just before the young woman was to move into the mansion her mother had built for her, on October 11, a courier came to Hampton. The mother had been busy that day because her daughter was away, taking a carriage down to Charleston for some shopping. The older Harriott met the messenger and called for a glass of sherry for him. He was weary after an obviously arduous ride. Harriott sat down to read the message.

Dearest Mother,

I have just eloped with Frederick Rutledge. Of course you know Frederick, a son of John, and a nephew of Edward, who signed the declaration declaring the colonies to be free and independent of England. Oh, Mother, you know how much I love Harrietta. It's so beautiful — it has your touch. You must find some use for it. Frederick and I shall live in his home in Charleston.

> Yours, with all the
> love in my heart,
> Harriott

October 11, 1797

Harrietta Plantation, the plantation built for an old maid, stood deserted for nearly sixty years.

The Legend of the Gray Man

There is a legend about the ghost that walks South Carolina beaches before each hurricane. When black clouds roll in from the southeast, and a sudden chill comes to the winds, a man in gray walks the beaches and by his very presence under the gathering clouds alerts those who see him to depart and take refuge in a safe place. It is said that no foghorn, lightship, or watchtower gives a more valid warning than the Gray Man.

THE LAST OF the rice crop was being harvested on the coastal South Carolina plantations in September 1822, and the families of the planters were still in residence at their houses by the seashore. As so many members of the planters' families had lost their lives because of malarial fever, brought on by mosquitoes that thrived in the low-lying rice fields, it was deemed dangerous for the families of the planters to remain on the plantations during the months that rice was being harvested. All of the planters maintained houses by the seashore or on offshore islands, where their families found a healthful, cool haven during August, September, and sometimes October.

During the first week in September 1822, a young man who had just returned to his home in South Carolina after spending two years abroad was flying along on his horse toward the beach at North Island, south of Pawleys Island. He was almost overcome with desire to see his fiancée, who was in residence at her father's beach house. The young man was accompanied by his manservant, who was pushing his horse to the peak of its endurance to keep up with his master.

As the young man on the horse came close to Middleton Pond, he spotted what he mistook to be a shortcut to the North Island beach. Without saying a word to his servant, with a slight movement of his hands and legs he moved his horse onto the pathway that led from the road. For a few minutes the horse ran steadily, his nostrils wide and flaring. Then the faithful steed stumbled and fell, and the young man was pitched through the air into the marsh. The horse tried to raise himself up but could not find footing. He had fallen into a mire of coastal quicksand.

The servant dismounted his horse quickly and searched for his master. The broad, muscular horse was thrashing about in the quicksand. The animal whinnied as the reddish brown of his sides and underparts sank out of sight.

A whimper suddenly brought the servant's attention to his master, who also was being sucked into a pool of quicksand. The servant ran to his horse, removed the bridle, and ran back to his master, throwing the bridle toward him. As the young man reached out, he became even more engulfed in the mass of extremely fine sand, and he could not grab the bridle. The servant ran to find a branch or anything to save his master. But when the servant returned to his master with a long branch, there wasn't even a ripple remaining where the man had floundered for his life. Just then the master's horse reared his head in a last effort

71

to save himself, and the servant watched as the horse disappeared in the sand. The hired man rode dejectedly to North Island and told the young girl that her fiancé had lost his life in the quicksand.

She was overcome with grief. Her father carried her upstairs and carefully laid her on her featherbed mattress. A physician was called.

The girl remained in her room for several days. Not even able to attend the memorial service for her fiancé, she took her meals as she reclined in the four-poster bed. Finally, her parents insisted that she get out of bed, dress herself, and go for a walk on the beach. She agreed to do so in an effort to boost her low morale.

While she was walking along the tideline in the late evening, suddenly, out of the sands, appeared the figure of her late fiancé, dressed in a somber gray suit. As she approached him, her arms outstretched, she recognized a characteristic gesture of his, a certain toss of the head, but she was more concerned with his expression. He seemed to be urging her to do something. His face showed extreme worry, and his forehead was wrinkled. As the girl ran toward him, her cheeks wet with tears, he disappeared into the mist.

That night, as she lay on the high four-poster bed, the girl dreamed that she was adrift in a turbulent and stormy sea in a small boat. Huge waves rocked the tiny craft, and salt water stung her cheeks and filled the boat. And then she saw her fiancé, dressed in gray, standing on the seashore, beckoning to her. And although she tried, she could not reach him. She was screaming and frantically trying to reach her fiancé as she awoke. Her father ran into the room, and the girl recounted the dream to him. "My fiancé was desperately trying to save me from disaster," she cried. "It

72

was so weird. He didn't call to me, but he seemed to be trying to save me from the storm." Her father considered what his daughter had told him and decided to leave North Island at once and take his daughter to Charleston, where she could be treated by a renowned physician.

Within an hour after they had left, a severe hurricane hit North Island. The homes of many islanders broke up, including the home of Robert Francis Withers, a prosperous rice planter. Withers managed to float to land on a piece of roof that remained buoyant, but his wife and three children were never found again.

On Debordieu Island, north of North Island, where the hurricane reached its height of destruction, two little twin girls, Anna and Charlotte Alston, were held up to an upstairs window by their nurse to view a house riding the waves, and the lights inside the house still glowed!

After the hurricane had abated, some people on Debordieu Island said they had seen a man in gray come ashore before the hurricane, and they felt a sense of warning emanating from him. Just after they saw the figure that came to be called the Gray Man, he disappeared into the sea mist.

There have been disastrous hurricanes to hit the South Carolina coast through the centuries. There was the great gale of 1804 and the two hurricanes of 1806, one of which blew down the lighthouse on North Island. But the most memorable of all were the hurricanes of September 1822, October 1893, and October 1954. It is legend that the Gray Man was seen prior to each of these three hurricanes, warning people to evacuate.

Does the Gray Man still exist to warn people of

disastrous hurricanes? No one knows, but there are many people who will evacuate the coast of South Carolina quickly if they see a man in gray walking along the beach.

Note: One person who saw the Gray Man was Bill Collins, an automobile dealer from Georgetown. It happened just before the October 1954 hurricane. Collins said he walked to his gazebo, built on a dune overlooking the ocean, and there he saw the Gray Man on the beach. Collins knew the legend of the Gray Man and immediately recognized him. The phantom disappeared while Collins was looking at him. He knew a hurricane was gaining momentum in the West Indies, but little did he know that Hurricane Hazel was swirling its way on a path toward Pawleys Island. Once certain of Hazel's path, Collins decided to evacuate.

Shortly after Collins and his family left the island, Hurricane Hazel thundered ashore, washing away houses and 30-foot dunes. But the Collins house was untouched. "Even the TV antenna did not blow down," said Collins, who added, "That's part of the Gray Man legend — that no harm comes to those who see him." (From 1954 newspaper reports.)

Dr. Buzzard Stands Trial

D R. B U Z Z A R D walked into the Charleston court-room with his lawyers and sat at a table before the presiding judge, who had just walked from his chambers, his black robe flowing about him. The witch doctor's shoulders were back, his head up, and he was wearing a white suit, white tie, white shirt, white spats, white shoes, and, as usual, purple sunglasses. If anyone had self-confidence, and confidence in the outcome of his case, it was Dr. Buzzard.

The other people in the courtroom had openly asked each other if it was known whether or not Dr. Buzzard was "chewing the root" on the judge, the solicitor, and the jury. Living in a remote area, surrounded by nature, Dr. Buzzard utilized roots and herbs found in the woodlands to control people around him. He often, in a kind of mystic rite, chewed a root that he called "snake root," and by chewing the root and affixing his stare, he tranquilized or "rooted" individuals who watched him.

It was also a matter of conjecture whether or not Dr. Buzzard had sprinkled dirt from a parson's grave, always taken at midnight, on the desks of the judge, the solicitor, and the sheriff. That dirt had "the power," according to Dr. Buzzard, and he could turn the decision of *any* jury and judge simply by sprinkling their chairs or desks with this dirt.

But on this day it seemed that Dr. Buzzard had not used the dirt and was not chewing the root. If that was true, Dr. Buzzard obviously didn't care if he was found guilty as charged. Could that possibly be true?

Dr. Buzzard had been the defendant in many court cases, and he always used his power from witchcraft to get himself out of trouble. He had always been found not guilty, even when everyone in the courtroom knew that he had committed the crime. But if Dr. Buzzard had "rooted" the court during this trial, none of the spectators or principals in the case knew about it.

Much of the emphasis of the testimony that followed during the days of Dr. Buzzard's trial was influenced by the realities of World War II. It was a time of great peril for the United States and its allies, and every man who was of draft age and in good health was expected to serve his country in uniform. The old South Carolina belief that all young men should be trained in the military arts and sciences was never stronger. Now that World War II was violently storming in Europe and the Pacific, it was expected that every young man, rich or poor, black or white, should be trained to serve in some capacity.

But it was a matter of fact that dozens of young men in and around Beaufort, South Carolina, were being rejected from the draft because of poor health, and in many cases it seemed that the young man had paid a visit to Dr. Buzzard the day before his physical examination to serve in the military service. It was, the prosecuting attorney pointed out, the objective of the court to prove that Dr. Buzzard had in some way helped these young men avoid being accepted as candidates for the armed forces.

As each young man followed another to the witness stand, it became clear that Dr. Buzzard had concocted two compounds that he could administer to them. It was not known what ingredients Dr. Buzzard put into his strange concoctions, but whatever the ingredients were, they resulted in the desired effect. If given one compound, the young man would suffer form high blood pressure during his physical examination, and if he took the other, he would suffer palpitations of the heart. After twenty-four hours had elapsed, ʰe would return to normal health.

As most of the people in the courtroom were filled with a sense of patriotism, Dr. Buzzard sensed an attitude of animosity toward him. The case against him was building, and desires were strong not only that Dr. Buzzard's practice on the young men come to an end but that he be punished severely as well.

Now and then Dr. Buzzard leaned forward and spoke to one of his attorneys, asking if the state had an airtight case against him. "It doesn't look good," one lawyer told him. And though each young man who was questioned as a witness against Dr. Buzzard was terrified, the state's case against Dr. Buzzard continued to build.

Finally, Dr. Buzzard took the witness stand. It was so quiet in the courtroom that you could almost hear the pulses of the people in the room.

"Do you practice witchcraft?" the prosecuting attorney asked Dr. Buzzard.

"Yes, I practice witchcraft," Dr. Buzzard answered precisely.

"Can you explain to the court some of the ways you practice witchcraft?"

"Well, I chew the root; in other words, I can root the court," Dr. Buzzard boasted.

"Would you please tell the court if you have, as you say, rooted the court on this day?"

"No. I have not rooted the court during this case," Dr. Buzzard answered.

There was a collective gasp in the courtroom, and the judge pounded his gavel nervously, calling for order in the courtroom.

"Other than rooting, can you enlighten us on other ways in which you practice witchcraft?"

"I place hexes and I remove hexes," Dr. Buzzard answered.

"And do you admit that you gave the young men who have appeared as witnesses in the courtroom mixtures that they say you blended and served to them to help them escape the draft into military service?"

Again the people in the courtroom were hushed, soundless.

"I do," Dr. Buzzard said with composure.

There was a common sigh in the courtroom, and the judge again pounded his gavel.

"What is Dr. Buzzard doing?" a spectator whispered to another. "He's admitting guilt."

"He knows what he's doing, and you better believe that," the other spectator answered. "Maybe he figures that if he admits guilt, he will retain more self-respect than if he denies it and is found guilty."

Later in the day, Dr. Buzzard was found guilty of collaborating with the young men to escape the draft. The judge leaned over his desk as he spoke to Dr. Buzzard, who now stood before him.

78

"I sentence you to five years in prison or a five-thousand-dollar fine."

Not even the remotest expression of remorse or surprise or resentment showed on Dr. Buzzard's face.

"Now, Dr. Buzzard," the judge went on, "I feel you will choose to pay the fine rather than serve the five years in prison. And I know that during these stringent war times, five thousand dollars will be difficult for you to put your hands on. Indeed, I think anyone would have difficulty in raising the money. For that reason, I am going to give you one week, seven days, in which to raise the money. But I want to make one thing clear. If you are not back here in one week with the five thousand dollars, you will be taken to prison to serve five years."

Dr. Buzzard looked the judge in the eye. "How do you want the money?" he asked casually.

"What do you mean?" the judge said.

Dr. Buzzard reached into the inside pocket of his coat and pulled out a large roll of bills held by a rubber band. He peeled off fifty, using his thumb. Then he put the roll back into his pocket.

There was pandemonium in the courtroom. People were laughing, cursing, but most of all, expressing disbelief. The judge stood up, pounding his gavel, calling for order. And as soon as the courtroom was hushed, Dr. Buzzard was heard to say, "Is cash all right?" as he handed the judge five thousand dollars.

The Ghost of the Headless Man

D RIVING ALONG THE avenue of oaks, you cannot see the plantation house at Wedgefield. But as you drive from under the canopy of low oak limbs draped with Spanish moss, there it is — between you and the Black River. The house is bright and fresh, but the surrounding ancient oaks, abandoned rice fields, and white cabins are remnants of a more genteel era.

In 1762 Samuel Wragg purchased 610 acres and named his property Wedgefield Plantation. The imposing manor house at Wedgefield was called one of the most beautifully designed and detailed Georgian homes in the United States by Michael Greer, the interior decorator for the White House during the time that Mrs. Kennedy was in charge of much of the restoration. Exquisite plaster moldings by the renowned craftsman, Pinckney of Charleston, adorned walls in the Wedgefield entrance hall. Moldings in the madam's bedroom were in the design of the Adam brothers, Scottish architects of the 1700s, and this room was referred to as "the most expensive woman's bedroom in the South."

A hierarchy in the slave population at Wedgefield was established when the plantation was begun. Of the one thousand slaves, the planter was the chief officer. The overseer came next. Then the driver. And so on. The person in charge of the rice fields was called the trunk minder. And so it was at Mansfield Plantation, adjacent to Wedgefield.

Mansfield also was noted for its beauty. Past the forest of pines, past six old brick bridges that span lagoons, and through a gateway (the gates are hung onto brick columns), you come to a street of slave cabins. Among them is a tiny, white chapel. A steeple reaches from the top of the wood building to moss-draped oak limbs, and adjacent to the chapel is a bell, hung in a simple frame tower. A little farther down the lane you see the winnowing house, high atop eight wood pilings. Rice was taken to the winnowing house and sifted through a sieve built into the floor. As the rice fell from the sieve to containers placed on the ground, the wind carried away the chaff. Beyond this old plantation building is a courtyard. From there a brick walkway, laid in the herringbone pattern, leads you to the manor house. It was during the time of the American Revolution that Mary Man and her husband, Archibald Taylor, invited people from Wedgefield Plantation to a party at Mansfield.

As the Wedgefield planter family was making preparations to go to Mansfield, the father and a daughter were quarreling, which was usual for them. The father had chosen not to side with the Colonies; his loyalties were with the Crown. He hated General Francis Marion, the Swamp Fox, and would do anything he could to hold back his progress, whereas the daughter was sympathetic with the Colonies and followed every move of the Swamp Fox. Now and then she found a way to send a message to General Marion, and although her father had not learned of it, she had sent word to Marion that her father was holding a friend of Marion's as a prisoner of the Crown. "We will all be going to a party at Mansfield," the girl wrote to Marion. "Even the Wedgefield guards will attend the party. But, should you choose to take advantage of the situation to release your friend, don't underestimate my father. He will surely post one of the sentries at the door to keep watch over the prisoner. However, I feel there will be no more than one guard watching the plantation and guarding the prisoner. I am responsible for the party being given at Mansfield, for it was my suggestion to my good friend Mary that we should bring the two families together for a little amusement with other friends and guests."

Whether or not Marion actually received the note, the girl did not know. But as she dressed for the party, she intensely hoped that Marion had received her letter and had made plans to act on the information she had given him.

At Mansfield, rice birds were being prepared for the feast. The tiny birds had been baked and split up the back and were now being broiled. When these birds were prepared correctly, no fork was used in eating them. The neck was held by the left hand, and the little right leg was held by the right hand. Also being prepared for the party were roasted and boiled turkeys, fish, oyster pie, and ham, which would be carved before serving. Rice and hominy, which were served at almost every plantation meal, were set aside to await last-minute cooking, and green peas and sweet potatoes would be served with thick butter. Colorful jellies, in cut-glass bowls, had been placed on the mahogany sideboard, and desserts consisted of orange pie, apple fritters, groundnut cheese cake, rice flour puffs, and transparent pudding. All of this would be washed down with claret, port, brandy, champagne, and madeira, all in great plenty.

It took several carriages to transport the Wedgefield family and guards to Mansfield. As the carriages rolled away from Wedgefield mansion a sentry with a rifle stood on the circular brick steps. The master of Wedgefield looked back through a small window at the rear of his carriage. The guard lifted a hand, and the master waved to him.

Other carriages arrived at Mansfield at the same time the Wedgefield coaches stopped at the mansion. Footmen helped people out of the carriages, which were then escorted away by plantation slaves. The Wedgefield entourage, except the Wedgefield guards who joined their counterparts from Mansfield at a party in a building near the mansion, was met at the door by a butler and ushered through the drawing room to the ballroom beyond. A quartet of string musicians from the plantation slave quarters played in a far corner. Groups of people stood around chatting.

Then the guests were summoned into the dining room, where the feast would be served, and each person was handed a crystal glass containing chilled champagne. The host of Mansfield, a patriot, held his glass up for a toast. But just before he gave the toast, the master of Wedgefield held up his glass and said, "To the King!" Suddenly everyone in the room became deathly quiet.

The host, his glass still high in the air, countered, "To the Colonies, and to their success in winning a lasting independence and peace from the Crown." Except for the master of Wedgefield, all the people cheered.

As the guests made their way down the buffet table, the two main topics of conversation among the men were the war and the cultivation of rice. The women talked of samplers they were embroidering, some in cross-stitch, and praised the fine tableware of silver and pewter that had come from England. The men got around to discussing the practicality of planting grapes for wine. Finally, the guests had finished the meal, and there was still much food on the tables. It was a custom of planter hosts always to provide a great deal more food than was needed in order to appear prosperous and unselfish.

During the evening, if any of the guests was preoccupied, it was certainly the daughter of the master of Wedgefield. She wondered what was going on back at Wedgefield Plantation. Was the prisoner still in custody? Had Marion acted on her suggestion in the letter?

It was a glorious night at Wedgefield as the sentry stood on the steps, looking up at the sky. The moon was shining on the pines and casting shadows from the moss that gently swung from the oaks. While the guard was lazily looking about, a group of Marion's men galloped up. Their horses braced to a stop, and a saber-wielding cavalryman jumped off his horse, ran up the steps, and in a flash whacked off the head of the surprised guard with one blow. Another cavalryman had already run past the first one into the house, calling the name of the prisoner. The prisoner responded from the room in which he was locked and tied and was rescued. Within minutes it was over, and all was quiet at Wedgefield.

When the Wedgefield family returned from the party at Mansfield, to their horror they found the headless sentry lying in a pool of blood on the front steps. Yet his head was nowhere in sight.

Seven weeks later, the daughter was roused from sleep by the sound of hooves crunching to a stop in front of the mansion's steps. She ran to her bedroom window, held the curtains apart, and looked into the yard. It was dark except for the steps, where a night lamp burned. Somewhere a dog barked. But there was nothing unusual there that she could see. And then a headless sentry tottered down the steps and into the yard. And just as suddenly as he had appeared, he disappeared.

Months later the same ghost appeared, only this time other members of the family saw the headless guard staggering around the yard in the gleam of moonlight. Was he looking for his head? It was speculated that he was.

Wedgefield Plantation has changed hands many times since the night the sentry lost his head. It has belonged to the Parkers, to the Reverend Francis H. Lance, rector of All Saints Episcopal Church at Pawleys Island, and to numerous other people. Throughout the years there have been many accounts of the headless guard lurching about the steps and yard looking for his head.

During April 1975, the Wedgefield manor house burned. Only the extreme left and right wings and the front facade remained. The roof caved in just behind the front of the house. The mansion was reconstructed on the site to match exactly the former house in beauty and charm, but the headless corpse was apparently a part of the former house, for he has never been seen again.

The Girl Who Was Buried Standing Up

T EN SLAVES FACED their master. They were loyal, but exhausted, ready to drop. Could it be that he was actually asking them to do this bizarre thing? If what they were hearing was true, then surely he had lost his mind. For days now they had listened to the usually poised and tactful man rant and rave. He had walked hours on end from one side of the veranda to the other, hitting the palm of a hand with the fist of the other, prattling absurdities. He had closed himself inside the mansion and shouted so strenuously that it seemed sure his lungs would burst. Now, he was asking his faithful helpers who had stood by him through all of this to complete the strange task. If only, one whispered, they could go back three weeks and erase all that had happened since that day when the ship came.

The day had started off beautifully. The weather wasn't muggy as usual, but cool. The sun was bright, and the sky blue. The South Santee River was calm, and over on the ocean the water was blue, almost navy blue.

The master of the plantation had been leaning against a pillar on his veranda, having his first glass of bourbon for that day. A green sprig of mint floated on the liquid in the glass. As he sipped his drink, he looked out over the river, and he saw a ship there dropping anchor off his plantation, Peachtree. Soon, men came ashore in a longboat, and they appeared to be carrying something that was quite heavy.

The master of Peachtree rushed down to his dock and confronted the men. "What's this?"

"Mon Capitaine," a mate said, "we dare not keep this man on board. He is at death's door with scarlet fever."

"What do you expect me to do?" the master said, looking into the eyes of the young, handsome ship's officer, who was a very sick man.

"We want you to help this mate," one of the ship's hands said. "We'll return for him in three days."

Just then the master's beloved twelve-year-old daughter ran to the side of her father. "What is it?" the girl with long blond curls asked.

"A very sick man," her father answered.

"What is the malady?" the girl asked, as her innocent blue eyes looked into the searching-for-help eyes of the young officer.

"Scarlet fever," her father answered. "I think we dare not take him inside the house."

"Oh, but Father," the girl cried as she continued to look at the young man at her feet on the dock. "Of course we'll take him in. And we'll nurse him back to health."

"But I don't think in this case we should," the father said. "Scarlet fever . . ."

"What's that scripture you're always knocking into my head?" she asked. "It's from Proverbs. I remember now: *He that hath pity upon the poor lendeth unto the Lord; and that which he hath given will he pay him again.*"

"But this man's not poor; he's sick," the father answered.

"Oh, Father, it's all the same. He's poor in health." The girl stooped down and took one of the sick man's hands. "You'll be well again, you'll see," she said lovingly.

"Don't touch him again!" the father screamed at his daughter. "Do you not realize this man has scarlet fever? Look at his skin. It already has red blots."

"He's cold. His temperature has dropped," the girl said softly. "And his pulse is rapid." The expression on the man's face indicated he was having pain and was in general distress.

"Get away, I say," her father commanded. "You know that you have always been susceptible to diseases associated with a bad throat. Go and get Cudjo and Beaver. Tell them to come at once. If you cannot find them, then get Bonapart. Get somebody! And tell your mother about this, but tell her to stay away from the sick man."

The girl ran for help, and when she returned with two slaves, the scarlet rash was spreading. Just then, the sick man lapsed into a coma. The master of the plantation had the slaves take the young officer to the Sick House, a building in the center of a row of slave cabins in which sick slaves were treated.

The next day the girl, against her father's strong orders not to do so, went to the Sick House. "That man from the ship," Cinchy, a nurse, said, "he's done passed. We got him in back of the Sick House on the coolin' board."

The daughter, deeply despondent, tears in her eyes, returned to the house and told her father of the young man's death. The father called for some of his slave helpers and told them to bury the man in the burying ground in the forest, the place where the slaves were buried. "When the ship returns, we will have to tell them the bad news," the master said. But the ship did not return on the day it was expected.

Ten days later, the master's daughter showed all the symptoms of scarlet fever. She was put to bed in her upstairs bedroom. Her father was delirious with anger. "The very indignity of the people on that ship bringing their sick officer here, exposing my daughter to the dreaded disease," he shouted. He sent for not one doctor, but three. When the doctors arrived, they administered medicines to the deathly sick girl. The house servants scurried upstairs and downstairs, doing what they could. The father railed loudly in his high-pitched voice, pacing back and forth on the veranda. The mother, full of agony, sobbed softly into her lace handkerchief at the foot of her daughter's bed.

When two of the physicians left the plantation (one remained with the patient), the father screamed at the servants to go to the neighboring plantations and tell the owners about his daughter's illness and ask them if they knew of anything that could help her. The servants went to Romney, Peafield, Woodville, Harrietta, Washoe, The Wedge, Waterhon, Wambaw, and Hampton plantations, and the masters of all these plantations came to Peachtree to try to help the master and his wife in their misery, offering them sympathy. But they knew of no magic healing medicine, and within three days, the girl was dead.

The father paced back and forth on the veranda for more than twelve hours. Then he barricaded himself and his wife with his daughter's body in the house and prevented anyone from entering. The slaves could hear him shouting inside. Neighbors came in carriages with the roofs draped in black cloth, but they were turned away at the gate.

With his own hands the father built the coffin, and he alone prepared the body for burial. When the body was in the coffin and ready for burial, the master of Peachtree sent for ten of his favorite slaves. They stood before him as he spoke to them. In his deranged state, he told them to go into the heart of his favorite tract of wooded land, a spot high above the river. He told them to set the coffin upright on the ground so that his daughter would be in a standing position. "Cover it with earth," he instructed. Then he spoke directly to Cudjo. "You are the one who has planted the gardens and made this plantation the showplace that it is. I want you to be responsible for the mound of earth over my daughter's coffin. Plant the most fragrant of flowers over her, and keep watch over the mound always. My daughter must never be alone."

But when the time came for the slaves to move the coffin into the grove of oak trees, the father could not allow another to touch it. He alone carried the coffin on his shoulders to its final resting place, and he alone held it in place as Cudjo piled earth around it. The mound of earth reached fifteen feet in height. Then Cudjo planted the site.

Hackberry and sugarberry plants formed a circle around the mound. Hollies formed an outer circle, and beyond the hollies was an orbit of camellias. Cape jasmine covered the mound. Spanish moss, tree ferns, and mistletoe were abundant in overhanging limbs. No more beautiful spot was nurtured in the woodlands of a South Carolina plantation, and so it remained until recent years.

90

Jack's Psychological Warfare

J ACK COULD SWIM farther and faster than any other person on the plantation. The master was proud that Jack was such a good swimmer. One day the master told Jack that he had placed a bet on him with the owner of Wachesaw Plantation. "Tomorrow a man is coming to swim against you. You're going to swim the Waccamaw River, going upstream."

"Upstream?"

"Yes. And what's more, you're going to swim upstream when the tide is going out. My money's riding on you swimming farther than he can."

"Yes, sir," Jack said, but he was thinking about how difficult it would be to swim against the tide to win the bet for his master. But what could he say? The master had placed the bet, and he knew he had to win.

The next day the master came to Jack's cabin. "You don't have to work in the fields today, Jack. I want you to be in good shape when the fellow who's going to swim against you from Wachesaw gets here. Just remember, you've got to swim farther upstream than he does."

The master left the cabin and Jack tried to rest, but he couldn't settle down and relax. All he could do was worry. Would the master punish him if he lost the bet, he wondered.

After a while a man came ambling down the road. He was tall and lean, and his muscles glistened in the sun. Jack went out to meet him. "Are you the man who's going to swim against me?"

"What do you mean *swim*?" the man asked. "I'm just going to float along and watch you struggle."

Jack walked beside the man in the hot sun, appraising his opponent as they went to the big house, his mind searching for a plan. Was there anything he could do or say to destroy the cockiness of his opponent?

The master came out of the big house just as the owner of Wachesaw Plantation rode up on his stallion. He shook hands with him, with Jack's opponent, and then with Jack. "You'll start from that log there," he said, pointing, "when I fire my pistol from the dock upstream. May the best man win." In an aside, he whispered to Jack, "And that had better be you!"

Jack's master and the owner of Wachesaw Plantation then rode off in the direction of the dock, leaving Jack and his opponent alone. A plan had come to Jack's mind, but he wasn't sure it would work. Still, he had to try it. He had to do something, and he had to do it quick. He was too afraid of losing to this muscular opponent.

"The tide is not quite at full flood," Jack said. "While we wait for the tide to turn and start going out, I'm going over to my cabin. I'll be back in a few minutes."

"Don't run out on me," his tall rival said with a smirk.

The tide turned, and it was the time for the race to begin. Jack came from his cabin and descended the river bank to where his adversary was waiting. He was toting a stove and a sack with grits, meal, meat, and lard. "Strap these things to my back," Jack said matter-of-factly to his competitor.

"What's all this stuff for?"

"You don't think I'm a fool, do you?" Jack asked with all the self-confidence in the world. "You don't think I'm going to swim that far upstream, and against the tide, without something to eat, do you?" he hooted.

With that, the tall man's eyes widened, and then he turned and scurried up the river bank and barefooted his way down the road toward his own plantation as fast as he could go.

"I don't know how fast or how far that fella can swim," Jack said to himself as he watched his competitor kick up little clouds of dust running down the road, "but he sure can run."

"Look! It's Alice, the Ghost!"

CLARKE A. WILLCOX opens The Hermitage, his Murrells Inlet waterfront home, once a week during spring, summer, and fall for visitors to see the home of the late Alice Flagg. Alice lived in the house until her death in 1849, and the lovely girl is said to appear at the home she loved so dearly and at the gravesite in the All Saints Church Cemetery near Pawleys Island, where Willcox says she was buried. Willcox's guests usually move on to the burial site after they have listened to the haunting and heartbreaking love story of Alice, the beautiful girl who died more than a hundred and thirty years ago.

"It was in 1981 that some girls came to see me," Clarke A. Willcox said, as he talked of a group of students who came to try to establish contact with Alice, the ghost of The Hermitage. Willcox rocked on the porch of The Hermitage. The only things between him and the creek were the white pillars that support the roof of the porch and the moss-draped oaks in the garden. A vast salt marsh and the ocean were in the distance. "They were lovely girls, students at Queens College in Charlotte. They were studying extrasensory perception. They had no reason in the world to make the story up about seeing Alice, and I believe it perfectly.

"For years we have had teen-agers, and older people too, come here to hear the story of Alice Flagg. They tour the house, and then they go down to the cemetery at All Saints Church where Alice was buried. If they go down there and think of it all as a joke, they don't have any experience at all," Willcox said. "But if they go thinking about Alice, grieving with her about her sad, short life, they do feel her presence in a great way. Some of them actually see her."

A counselor who accompanied the fifteen Queens students to Murrells Inlet told them he believed if anyone could be tuned in to the channel of communication with a ghost, surely they could. In the van on the way to Murrells Inlet, some of the students worried that the trip would be wasted, that the ghost would not be revealed to them. "Look at it this way," the counselor said. "We'll enjoy the trip anyway. It isn't all that far away, and the weather is lovely. If we don't actually see Alice of The Hermitage, we will at least have had a nice one-day field trip to the coast of South Carolina."

They arrived at Murrells Inlet and turned at the old brick gates under huge live oaks into the road that led to The Hermitage. Mr. Willcox greeted them on the porch of the gleaming white frame house facing the creek, marsh, and ocean beyond. Someone asked him about the ancient brick from which the walkway and steps had been made.

"The brick came here as ballast in ships coming from England during the eighteen hundreds," he explained. "After it was unloaded, rice was taken aboard and the ships returned to England." After he called their attention to the virgin pine columns that support the porch roof, they all went inside. Willcox showed them through the house, explaining that it had been constructed by slaves and took four years to build. Upstairs they went into the bedroom that had been occupied by Alice Flagg. A soft breeze blew in from the ocean, and lace curtains danced in and out with the breeze. No one could feel that Alice's presence was in the room.

"What about the site in All Saints Cemetery, where Alice was buried?" one of the girls asked. "Would we be likely to see Alice there?"

"Possibly," Willcox said. Then he explained that inside the old brick wall of the cemetery at All Saints Church they would find a flat marble slab with one word carved on it — ALICE. "If you are really serious about seeing Alice in the cemetery," he said, "you should walk backward around the grave thirteen times, preferably with your eyes closed. Then you can wait for Alice to make her presence known to you."

The students and their counselor got back into their van and drove via US 17 to Pawleys Island, then turned off US 17 to the right onto SC 255 and traveled about two and a half miles west of Pawleys Island, where they found the old church in a grove of trees, surrounded by a wall of old brick.

For a time they looked around the beautiful old church that had been the chief galvanizing agent of the planters. The planters were all Episcopalians, as the rectors did not condemn slavery, and it was at church that they got news of their neighbors, the latest political information, and tidings of England. They usually brought Sunday dinner in baskets and ate in the grove of trees after the Sunday worship services.

The students spread out and wandered through the cemetery. "Here it is, Alice's grave!" one of them shouted. Limbs of a tree hung low over the grave identified with only one word — ALICE. All the girls came to stand around Alice's grave.

"Shall we each walk around it backward, thirteen times?" one of the girls asked.

"Absolutely," the teacher said. "That's why we're here. To do everything we can to try to communicate with the ghost."

Each girl walked around the grave backward thirteen times with her eyes closed. Sometimes the other girls would have to give instructions to keep the student in the path that led around the grave marker. "Just keep walking in the sand where there's no grass," one girl explained. "There's grass in the cemetery except right here around Alice's grave."

After the students had finished this ritual, they continued to stroll about the cemetery. After a while they made their way to the back of the cemetery, where they all looked over the brick wall at a pond of stagnant water. Cypress trees grew in the pond, and long-winged insects flew just over the surface of the fetid water. Just then a beautiful girl in a flowing white dress with a wide ruffle walked up to the girls, holding one hand over her chest. She didn't speak.

"Who is that?" one of the girls asked another.

"I don't know. She must have come out of those camellia bushes over there."

When the girl in the white dress jumped effortlessly over the wall and disappeared into the swamp water, one of the students screamed. "It was Alice, the ghost!"

At that very moment the girls realized they had seen Alice. They waited for a while to see if the vision would appear again, and then they left the cemetery to make arrangements to spend the night on Pawleys

Island so they could visit the cemetery again the next day.

It was the afternoon of the following day, after a sleepless night discussing what they had seen, that the students again went to the All Saints Church Cemetery. It made sense, they reasoned, to go at about the same time they had gone the day before. Perhaps Alice made a visit to her place of burial at the same time each day.

When they went through the heavy iron gate and came to the grave, they decided that, just as they had done the day before, each one would walk around Alice's grave backward thirteen times with her eyes closed. After they had done this, they went to the wall at the back of the cemetery, where they could see the swamp into which Alice had disappeared the day before. Suddenly, Alice appeared right in front of them, sitting on the brick wall, dangling her feet. For some reason, the girls became so frightened that they all ran back toward the center of the cemetery. All except one girl, named Mary. Mary remained at the wall, staring at Alice.

"Please, Mary," a friend called. "Come here."

But Mary didn't seem to hear her friend.

Then another friend called. "Mary, for heaven's sake, come here. You're standing too close to the ghost."

Mary, walking slowly, her head high, her eyes seemingly looking toward the sky, turned and walked toward Alice's grave. She stopped at the head of the grave marker.

"Mary, come on now," the counselor coaxed. "Come over here where we are. Over here under the big tree."

But Mary didn't seem to hear as she stood by the grave of Alice Flagg.

Then the ghost of Alice jumped down off the wall and started walking toward Mary. When she came close to her, Mary held out a hand, but it went right through the space where the girl in the white dress was standing. As she looked at Mary, Alice Flagg rose gently into the air, floated over her grave, and dreamlike, sank into it.

Mary fainted, falling over Alice's grave. The girls and the counselor ran to her, trying to revive her. When Mary did awaken, she seemed to be in a trance, and she talked in an unknown tongue. Mary didn't recover fully until she arrived at school in Charlotte.

"That's exactly how it happened," Willcox finished. "One of the girls came back here and told me all about it. I have no reason in the world not to believe her."

Note: Clarke A. Willcox is the author of *Musings of a Hermit*.

Shaking the Dust

A FTER THE TURN of the twentieth century, a
group of Pentecostal Holiness people traveled to
the coast of South Carolina in an effort to establish a
church and expand the number of members of their
religious denomination. They decided to study two
coastal counties and choose between the two.

They first considered Georgetown County, examining the events that might shape the course of the
future and the events that dealt with the past. Many of
the people of Georgetown County were descendants
of the rice planters whose fortunes had been accumulated on the plantations along the coastal rivers. These
rivers had supplied the means with which to create a
culture and style of living unusual in colonial America.

The planter families had lived almost like the royal
families of Europe. They vacationed abroad. Most of
them maintained houses in Charleston for the winter
social seasons. They imported from New England and
Europe governesses and tutors for their children.
Slaves attended to their every need. There were dog-
minders and cat-minders, a fly-brush boy to wave
away flies, a servant in a plantation manor house to
handle the task of opening and closing windows, and
another to take care of the small area of garden where
mint was grown, the mint to be used in juleps.

Homes of the planters contained furniture brought from Europe or pieces made in the popular European styles by artisans on the plantation. Fine china and crystal came from England. Abundant fish and game in the coastal area added variety to the bounteous harvests from the plantations, and at lavish dinners, fine imported wines accompanied the food.

As Episcopal rectors did not condemn slavery, planters were mainly Episcopalians, and many of their descendants continue to support the Episcopal churches with their membership, service, and money even today.

After taking all of this into consideration, the Pentecostal Holiness people next studied the residents of neighboring Horry County during the period of time that Georgetown County was considered to be one of the country's most prestigious addresses. They learned that at that time the people of Horry County were considered poor and primitive, but they were willing to work for something better, sustained by hope and courage. The Pentecostal Holiness folk liked that trait about the people of Horry County, but they continued their study of the two counties.

What was the factor that had caused such a difference in the lifestyles of the people of the two side-by-side counties, they wondered. They learned it was the ocean tides. Rivers that flowed through Horry and Georgetown counties and emptied into the sea received the tidal flow from the Atlantic Ocean. But the rise of the tide, although it extended for a distance inland, encompassing Georgetown County, did not include Horry County. And so it was that the people of Georgetown County lived on land that had the "proper pitch of the tide" that enabled the fields

101

adjoining the rivers to be flooded and drained as tides rose and fell. More than two hundred plantations were built in Georgetown County, and every inch of land bordering the rivers was planted in rice, tended by slave labor.

While the people in Georgetown County were cultivating rice and accumulating fortunes that elevated them to the ranks of the richest in the land, the people in Horry eked out their living in the forests, which yielded lumber and turpentine. Turpentine was taken from the pine trees in much the same way that maple sap was taken from sugar maple trees in New England. Men cut the pine bark away with a special tool, and the thick, gummy sap was collected in cups. The sap was then boiled in a vat. Tar, another product of the pine trees, was obtained by the distillation of pine wood. Pitch, which was used in the making of boats, was also manufactured in Horry County. Pitch was made by boiling tar in round clay holes in the earth.

The people of Horry County were predominantly of the Methodist denomination, because Bishop Francis Asbury, a pioneer Methodist minister, had ridden his horse from settlement to settlement during the late 1700s and preached to the people.

The Pentecostal Holiness folks weighed the situation: should they settle among the Episcopalians of Georgetown County or the Methodists of Horry County? They finally chose Horry County because they liked what they had learned about the people there and they believed Methodists would be more down-to-earth and friendly than the well-to-do Episcopalians. When they moved into Horry County, they were not prepared for the rebukes they received from the loyal and faithful Methodists, who would no more become Pentecostal Holiness followers than they would become worldly-wise Episcopalians like the people of Georgetown County!

When the Pentecostal Holiness people realized that they were being received only with cold disapproval in Horry County and that their reception, should they go there, would be no better in Georgetown County, they held a meeting to decide what to do. It was clear that they were wasting their time and efforts to become a part of the coastal community, and there was nothing to do but move away. But they did not intend to leave Horry County without making it well known that they had not been accepted by the people of the county.

They packed their bags, went to the small village of Adrian, and placed a pine box in the middle of the crossroad, the most conspicuous place in the small town.

The leader of the Pentecostal Holiness group stepped up on the pine box, as the others crowded around and recited the scripture to which they had turned for guidance, Mark 6:11:

And whosoever shall not receive you,
nor hear you, when ye depart,
shake off the dust under your feet
for a testimony against them.

As each person repeated the words of the scripture, speaking very solemnly, that person shook each foot forcefully, as though shaking the dust as testimony against the people of the town of Adrian and Horry County.

Note: A Pentecostal Holiness church was established in Horry County just prior to World War II, and its members were cordially welcomed. Today there are several fine Pentecostal Holiness churches in Horry County, and Horry County is the richest county in the state primarily because of tourism.

The Diamond Watch

M ARIAH LIVED on Racepath Avenue in Conway, but she worked as a maid for Mrs. Beasley
on Mrs. Beasley's plantation just outside of town. The
plantation was not the well-kept home and landscaped
grounds that it once had been, but Mrs. Beasley had
been able to hold onto her estate, and she retained
some of the things she had inherited from her ances-
tors.

One day Mrs. Beasley told Mariah that she didn't
feel very well. Mariah helped Mrs. Beasley lie down,
and the maid sat by the bed and applied hot cloths to
Mrs. Beasley's forehead.

"Mariah, I feel like I might die," Mrs. Beasley said.
"You have been good to me. I want to give you
something to remember me by."

"You don't have to do nothin' like that," Mariah
protested.

"I know I don't, but I want to. Bring me my jewelry
box."

Mariah went to the other side of the room and got
the ornate box that always sat on the top of the bureau.
She put it on the bed where Mrs. Beasley could reach
it.

Mrs. Beasley opened the box and removed a round,

gold, diamond-studded watch with a gold chain. Shafts of sunlight came through the ceiling-to-floor windows and reflected a blaze of blue, green, red, and gold from the diamonds as the woman held the watch in her hand.

"Here, take the watch," Mrs. Beasley said as she handed it to Mariah. "I have given you a few things before, but they were just clothes that I had no use for, and some other things that were of no value. This watch is something of value. I want you to have it."

Mariah hardly knew what to do. She extended a hand, then withdrew it, as though she couldn't really accept the diamond watch. Then she held out both hands, and Mrs. Beasley dropped the watch into them.

"Oh, Miz Beasley," Mariah said, "you sure?"

"Yes. I am very sure, Mariah."

That night Mariah told her husband about the watch. She had put it in a bureau drawer.

"Let me see it," her husband said.

Mariah got the watch, and she and her husband examined it in the light from a lamp. There were no diamonds in the neck chain, but the face of the watch was encircled in a double row of diamonds. Mariah's husband estimated the watch to be comprised of at least forty stones. Although there was an almost magical radiance about the watch, never once did Mariah put the watch around her neck.

After Mariah had put the watch away, her husband said to her, "You know, I don't think you should show that watch to none of our friends."

"Why?"

"Someone could rob us. That's just what it would

106

take to get robbed. For someone to know that 'spensive watch's in this house."

"Oh, I don't think so," Mariah reasoned. "I think our friends would be glad Miz Beasley gave me this watch."

"That thing's worth a lotta money," Mariah's husband said. "Watcha gonna do with it?"

"I don't know," Mariah answered. She hadn't really thought about it. It was a beautiful watch, but she couldn't wear it. What would everybody say? They had never seen such a thing before. She liked to wear the shiny cross she had gotten at the five and dime a lot. Anyway, if she ever wore the watch, it would only be to church, and she would much rather wear the cross there.

Mariah thought about the diamond watch some more, and she decided that maybe her husband was right. Someone might think of robbing them. She'd better hide the watch. But where would she hide it?

Mrs. Beasley had given Mariah some old clothes which she kept on a shelf in the room they called the spare room. Mariah went to the spare room and looked at the things Mrs. Beasley had given her. There were a coat and two dresses, stuffed into a shopping bag. Mariah hadn't taken the clothes out of the bag since Mrs. Beasley had given them to her. And there was also a vase, and then there were the bowl and pitcher. She would, she thought, keep the diamond watch with those things. If she put it in the vase, someone would probably think to look there if they were robbed. The bowl and pitcher provided no safety either, she thought. Then she saw a pair of shoes that Mrs. Beasley had given her. They were pushed way back on the shelf. Mariah slipped the watch into the pointed toe of a black leather shoe. She wasn't even going to tell her husband where she had put the watch. It would worry him, and he would think a lot about being robbed.

Mariah's husband must have thought about the diamond watch all the time, for he kept telling her to get rid of it before they got robbed. After all, he surmised, their house had only three rooms, the living room, which also served as a bedroom, the kitchen, and the spare room. It would be easy to rob such a house, he explained.

"Who in the world would think we had anything they'd want to rob us for?" Mariah asked him. "This house has never had a coat of paint, and the roof is in need of repair. Nobody would want to break in here."

One day Mariah saw a dress at Bailey Blanton's Department Store. It was exactly what she would like to have to wear to church on Mother's Day. And it was just her size, size 18. Her church always had a special program on Mother's Day, and every mother in the congregation was asked to stand up and give testimony on the virtues of being a good mother. Mariah thought she couldn't stand it if she couldn't buy that dress to wear to church on Mother's Day. But Mariah didn't have much money. She had never charged Mrs. Beasley very much because she knew that Mrs. Beasley lived on her social security and had to pay a lot of taxes on her plantation. Mariah sneaked a look at the price tag. Why, that dress costs sixty-eight dollars! Mariah had never paid sixty-eight dollars for a dress in her life. It was right at that moment that Mariah thought about the watch at home in the shoe. How much could she get for the watch, she wondered.

That night at supper Mariah's husband said he would give anything in the world to have a tiller with which to plow the garden. He'd had a hard time plowing since his old mule, Tony, had died.

"How much would a tiller cost?" Mariah asked.

"Oh, I don't rightly know," he said. "Guess 'bout three hundred dollars. Next time I'm up at Sears I'm gonna look at one."

Mariah thought about that. If she sold the diamond watch, would it bring in enough for her to have the dress and her husband to have a tiller? She went to the spare room to take a look at the watch.

Lo and behold, the things that Mrs. Beasley had given Mariah were gone!

"Where's them things?" Mariah screamed to her husband.

"What things?"

"Them things Mrs. Beasley done give me!"

"Oh, them things. A lady from the church wanted some things what could be sold at a garage sale. She took them."

Mariah sighed as she thought about the watch in the shoe. She couldn't rightly blame her husband for giving the things away. He didn't know the watch was in the shoe, and she had never paid much attention to the things on the shelf in the spare room.

"When did she come?" Mariah asked her husband.

"Yesterday."

"Who was it?"

"I think it was Sister Brown."

The next day, after Mariah got home from Mrs. Beasley's, she went to the home of Sister Brown and asked her if she had the things her husband had given her.

109

"Why, yes," Sister Brown said. "They're still in my car."

"Would you mind if I took the shoes back?" Mariah asked.

"No," Sister Brown said.

"The two women went to the back of the house, where Sister Brown's car was parked. Sister Brown unlocked the trunk of her car, lifted the lid, and there were the things that had been on Mariah's shelf in the spare room. Mariah lifted the shoes out of the trunk of the car, and while she was talking to Sister Brown, she slipped a finger into the toe of a shoe. There it was! The watch was still inside the shoe. Glory be!

"Thank you. Thank you so much," Mariah said, and then she hurried back to her house. She didn't tell her husband about the watch and how close she had come to losing it. To him the watch was just something to worry about.

Mariah didn't think much about the watch for about a year. Mrs. Beasley's health had improved, and Mariah's work at the plantation wasn't as hard as it used to be. One day while Mariah was shopping at Bailey Blanton's Department Store, she saw another dress, much like the one she had seen the previous year. Bless my soul, Mariah thought, there's another dress like I want. She lifted the hanger and took the dress to a window where the light was good. Size 18. But the price was seventy-two dollars. Oh, my, she thought, I can't pay that much for a dress. She took the dress back to the rack. That was more than last year's dress. She thought about her husband's garden and how much he needed a tiller to help him get the soil plowed up.

Filled with determination, Mariah marched down

110

the street to the Bright Gem Jewelry Store. She told the manager about the watch and asked him what he would give her for it. He said he would have to see the watch; he couldn't give her an appraisal without examining the watch. He didn't take much time with her, and he acted as if he didn't believe she had a watch, as she said, with real diamonds.

Mariah raced home, got the watch from the shoe, and went back to the jewelry store. The manager, not known for his honesty, examined the watch. He licked his lips. "Hmmmm," he said. "You know, Mariah, diamonds aren't bringing very much right now." He held the watch up. "The chain is gold. Let me see. I guess I could give you about, oh, I don't know. Let me see."

Mariah did a little calculating in her head. The dress was about eighty dollars and the tiller would be about three hundred. "Would you give me three hundred and eighty dollars?"

"Oh, no, Mariah. Why, this watch would bring you something more in the range of, let me see, oh, about one hundred seventy-five."

Mariah reached out and grabbed the watch. "Well, that's not enough."

Back home, Mariah put the watch back in the toe of the shoe. That night she told her husband about going to see the jeweler. He stared at her as she explained that what she really needed was money, not a diamond watch.

"Why did you do it, Mariah?"

"Do what?"

"Take that watch and show it to that man? Don't you know that now we will be robbed? Don't you have no sense a-tall?"

111

"That man don't even know where we live," Mariah said in defense.

"You better believe he knows now," the husband said. "He'll make it his business to find out." Then Mariah's husband held out the palm of a hand, and as he talked he jabbed the palm with the forefinger of his other hand. "One thing's sure, and two things certain. Up to today, nobody knew 'bout the diamond watch but you and me and Miz Beasley. Now that jewelry man knows it, and the Lord only knows how many others knows about it." He shook his head in desperation. "We gotta get rid of that watch tomorrow."

That night Mariah didn't sleep very well. She had the fidgets in her legs and couldn't keep them still, and her husband's tossing around in the bed bothered her. Hour after hour, Mariah twisted around in the bed, stretching out, curling up; she couldn't get into a comfortable position at all. At about the time that she heard a rooster down at the barn crow, Mariah got out of bed. She sure was glad her husband didn't know where the diamond watch was, and she sure was glad daylight had finally come. As she cooked breakfast for her husband and herself, she could hardly keep from singing "Amazing Grace." She did hum that tune, quietly, as she worked. When her husband got up, a good breakfast was on the table, and after they had eaten the meal, Mariah cleaned up the kitchen and was on her way to Mrs. Beasley's plantation. All the way to the plantation, Mariah sang "Amazing Grace."

Mrs. Beasley was in the garden clipping roses. "My, them's pretty flowers," Mariah said as she walked up to Mrs. Beasley.

"Yes, they are pretty," Mrs. Beasley replied. "You

112

know, the earliest of the roses are always the most perfect ones."

"Uh, Miz Beasley," Mariah said.

"Yes?" Mrs. Beasley stopped cutting roses and turned toward Mariah.

"You know that diamond brooch you has? That one in your jewelry box that you never wears?"

"Why, yes, I remember that brooch, Mariah. Why?"

"Who you gonna give that to?"

Laudatory Notice

A FTER THE CIVIL WAR, Major John Jenkins returned to his plantation on Edisto Island. His dream was to plant sea island cotton and make a great deal of money in order that his son, George Washington Seabrook Jenkins, could attend Princeton, as had the other male members of the Jenkins family. The land was fertile that year, and all signs pointed to a good year for cotton.

With all of the changes wrought by the war, there was an eerie grandeur to Edisto Island. The fine, somewhat dilapidated houses were surrounded by bumpy, casually tended gardens. But no little girls in white muslin dresses played cheerfully in the gardens, as they had before the war, while their elders sat on the verandas arguing lazily about politics and discussing crops and the latest news from England.

Major Jenkins had no slaves and precious little in assets, but he had high hopes of regaining the fortunes that he had been accustomed to before the war. Edisto planters had accumulated riches from cotton that nearly matched the riches the Waccamaw planters had obtained from rice. Jenkins knew the old aristocracy would grasp new opportunities and become richer than before, while others would not be able to cope and would lose what little they had left after the war.

114

He was determined to become one of the planters who would adjust to the new regime, master the new relations with the former slaves, and thereby regain prosperity. He wanted it not only for himself and his wife but for his son, whom he called Washy. He explained this to Washy and told him that only a Princeton education could bring him "laudatory notice" from his fellowman.

Filled with passion for becoming a successful cotton planter, Major Jenkins borrowed a great deal of money for his venture. His vast lands became green with cotton plants, and, finally, the fields turned into great stretches of white cotton, ready for the harvest.

Then one night, a night that is still talked about on Edisto Island, millions of caterpillars descended on the fields of cotton. The caterpillars had strong, biting jaws and a ravenous appetite. The wormlike creatures guided themselves quickly about the cotton plants by pairs of short, jointed feelers, and by daybreak the heavy eaters had consumed all of the cotton. Jenkins not only lost his assets but was heavily in debt.

The following day, Major Jenkins told Washy that going to Princeton was out of the question. Washy explained that going to Princeton and receiving laudatory notice from his fellowman didn't mean everything in the world to him. He would be just as happy, or more, to remain on the island and receive no honors or awards.

From that day on Washy began what would become a lifelong love affair with the sea. In his small boat he went from one island to another. The wildlife on the islands fascinated him, and he felt at home in the dense groves of palmetto and live oak trees. There wasn't a foot of sand dune, salt marsh, maritime

115

forest, or island beach that he didn't explore if he could reach it by boat.

One day while on an abandoned, remote island, Washy heard a faint cry. He couldn't understand the words as they were not English, but the young man could tell that someone was in trouble. Going in the direction of the cry, he found a man lying under a large tree. Washy got him into the boat and took him to a young physician, who promised to do what he could to restore him to good health. Washy learned that the man's name was Antoine and that he had been a sailor on a passing vessel. When he became ill, his shipmates had taken him ashore and left him. They feared he had come down with cholera, and they didn't want to be exposed to that dreaded disease.

As Washy grew, so did his responsibilities and the size of his boats. He became captain of a tugboat and then later of a larger tugboat named *The Juno*, which traveled between Beaufort and Charleston. From time to time he thought about Antoine and wondered if he had regained his health.

One day an unexpected storm of much violence boiled in over the horizon, and Washy put to shore in *The Juno*. As he was tying up at the dock, he heard talk of a vessel in distress. It was *The Riga* bound for Tybee, Georgia, from Le Havre, France. A pilot boat, *The Charleston*, was in the vicinity but was unable to come to the aid of the sinking ship because of the nor'easter that was becoming more deadly with each gust of wind. "If I had a hand or two to go with me," Washy said, "I'd help that vessel in trouble." Two mates stepped out of a small building on the dock and volunteered to accompany Washy. To his amazement, one of the mates was Antoine. There was a fond

116

embrace between the two, and then with the other hand they put out to sea.

It was three men against the angry seas as they fought to keep *The Juno* on course. The waves loomed higher than the craft. To make matters worse, they were unable to locate the boat in distress. Finally, Washy turned the ship back toward the harbor. On the way, *The Juno* came alongside the British steamship *Kingdom*, and the officer in charge yelled that he could see the boat in trouble. It was breaking up.

Washy immediately turned *The Juno* around and headed out to sea. With each wave that crashed on the vessel, he was fearful that *The Juno* was going to break apart. And then he saw in the churning water people hanging onto pieces of wood and other debris, anything that was floating. They were crying out, begging for help. Washy and Antoine tossed lifelines to them and hauled them aboard *The Juno*. Without exception, each thankful survivor said that within a few more minutes he would have been unable to hold on.

Washy and his two mates on *The Juno* received citations from the King of Norway, under whose flag the distressed ship had been sailing. Washy was presented a gold medal of honor, awarded under the provisional Act of the U.S. Congress, and Antoine and the other hand were awarded silver medals similar to the gold one Washy had received. George Washington Seabrook Jenkins had not gone to Princeton, but he had received laudatory notice from his fellowman just the same because of his courage and knowledge of the sea.

The Minister and the Melons

T HE PEOPLE of the Baptist Church of Aynor looked for their preacher. It seemed that he had disappeared with an undetermined amount of money as well as the watermelons they had contributed to the church. The minister, money, and melons were all gone.

Aynor, a small town fourteen miles northwest of Conway, wasn't always the thriving community that it is today. During the early part of this century the people of Aynor worked hard in order to contribute money for the upkeep of their churches, and the town acquired a reputation for being a friendly, agricultural town. Annual parties and taffy pullings were held, and goobers were always served because they were grown abundantly in the area. Watermelon cutting was another social event held annually in Aynor, for fields of watermelons surrounded the village during the summer months.

Most of the people of Aynor belonged to the Baptist Church, and they had authorized their preacher to ship to Florida a carload of watermelons in his name. This was to be done on the premise that the church would receive the profits when payment for the melons was made. But a few days after the melons had been hauled to the church and turned over to the

118

preacher, the people could not locate him. A group of church people went to the postmaster to find out if he knew anything about the minister and the melons.

The postmaster vouched for the fact that he had indeed delivered the letter from the buyer of the melons to the preacher, but for the life of him he could not remember the name or address of the buyer.

The church people waited for several days longer, and then they came to the conclusion that if the clergyman had delivered the melons to the unknown buyer and had been paid for them, he had obviously absconded with the money. The church treasurer had not received a penny of it, nor could the preacher be found. There were no telephones in the community at this time, and no one could come up with an address where they could write to get information on the whereabouts of the preacher.

Finally, the people of the Baptist Church gave up their search for the preacher and the money he had gotten from the sale of the watermelons. A new minister was selected for the church, and the congregation grew in number and in good fellowship, including church dinners for which they prepared and ate their famous chicken bog.

Several years passed, and a couple who had long been members of the Baptist Church planned a trip to Florida. As they were religious people and devoted to the worship of God, they stopped in Jacksonville on Sunday morning to attend services at a Baptist church. To their utter surprise, the minister who walked out to the pulpit was the very one who had once served the Baptist Church at Aynor and had disappeared with the watermelons. It was obvious that as soon as the minister came to the pulpit and looked out over the congregation, he recognized the couple from Aynor sitting in the pews. He turned pale, his hands trembled, and he seemed unable to speak clearly.

But when it came time for him to read the scripture, he seemed to gain confidence. Reading with determination, he spoke each word distinctly. When he came to the last sentence, he lifted his eyes from the Bible and looked directly at the couple from Aynor. They were the only ones who seemed to notice that a plea was spontaneously added to the scripture, Jeremiah 13:15–18:

> And if thou seeist me
> And recognizist me
> Hold your peace, *and*
> *I will talk with you.*

About the Author

NANCY RHYNE has traveled all over the world and has collected coastal folklore on three continents, Greece, and the British Isles. But her first love is the South Carolina coast, and she has written dozens of articles about the area, its history, and its legends. She is the author of two award-winning books, *Tales of the South Carolina Low Country* and *Carolina Seashells*. Rhyne lives with her husband in Myrtle Beach and teaches a course on South Carolina folklore at Coastal Carolina College in Conway.